WHERE

TOR BOOKS BY KIT REED

Enclave
The Night Children
The Baby Merchant
Dogs of Truth
Thinner Than Thou
@Expectations

W H E R E

Kit Reed

A TOM DOHERTY ASSOCIATES BOOK

NEW YORK

WHERE

Copyright © 2015 by Kit Reed

"Military Secrets" copyright © 2015 by Kit Reed. This story first appeared in the March 2015 issue of *Asimov's Science Fiction*.

Designed by Mary A. Wirth

A Tor Book
Published by Tom Doherty Associates, LLC
175 Fifth Avenue
New York, NY 10010

www.tor-forge.com

Tor® is a registered trademark of Tom Doherty Associates, LLC.

The Library of Congress Cataloging-in-Publication Data is available upon request.

ISBN 978-0-7653-7982-5 (hardcover)
ISBN 978-1-4668-7049-9 (e-book)

Tor books may be purchased for educational, business, or promotional use. For information on bulk purchases, please contact the Macmillan Corporate and Premium Sales Department at 1-800-221-7945, extension 5442, or write to specialmarkets@macmillan.com.

First Edition: May 2015

Printed in the United States of America

0 9 8 7 6 5 4 3 2 1

FOR DANIEL
FOR REALS

WHERE

1

David Ribault
Thursday, before dawn

If there was a shift in the skies at his back just then— any change in the wind to signify what was coming, Davy didn't know it. The islands were at his back, the skies ahead, dark as fuck. He was on the last causeway to the mainland, getting cranked up to confront Rawson Steele, object?

Deconstruction.

Look, the first time he saw the guy, he was stealing a car on Front Street— at least Davy thinks he was. Last week he caught this well-dressed stranger hotwiring a needle-nosed Lexus with out-of-state tags on the main drag. Nobody steals cars in downtown Charlton, South Carolina, at least not this early; nobody lays his classy suit jacket across the hood while he's doing it: flaunting Hugo Boss on Front Street at an hour when no tourists come.

Perfect hair. That suit. *Not from around here.*

Davy let it go by, but he unlocked his offices with the creepy feeling that he wasn't the first.

David Ribault's sense of order is profound. He can tell when something's wrong. An architect, he knows the location of everything in his office, down to the last pencil. He doesn't know how, he just knows how it is. It's what drove him to architecture in the first place. He wants to improve his part of the world with designs that can be set down and defined in terms of absolutes. It's about sorting out the mess and confusion of life, a least a little bit, with symmetry.

He studied the configuration of objects on his drafting table for too long, scowling. *Everything looks OK, but it isn't.* He couldn't pin it down, exactly. He just knew.

Don't be stupid, he told himself, but it was creepy.

Then, driving back to Merrill's neat little steamboat bungalow on Kraven island that night, he slammed on the brakes. The sleazy hotwire wizard's car crouched in the no-parking zone outside the Harbor City Inn, vibrating in place like a dog that somebody told, "Stay," and then forgot. Davy's back hairs bristled. *Not your car.*

He saw the driver stalking up the walk to the hotel like he owned the place. However he charmed Martha Ann Calhoun at the desk, whatever he had to pay her, days have passed and that car is still sitting there. Did the big-city stranger come back and turn off the motor or did he leave it running in place until the tank burned dry?

"That car? It belongs to this big gun from New York, his name is Rawson Steele," Merrill said when he came home fuming. "We had a great conversation."

Davy's back went up. "Stay away from him, he's a sleazeball."

She shut him down with a silky smile. "Well, he was very nice to me."

So Steele hit on Davy's girl before he even knew it, worked his dark magic before he could go, *watch out.* Everybody knows him now, Kraventown is that small. He knifed his way in here like a tiger shark hunting in the swash, finds a way to get in your face, standing too close with that innocent fuck-me grin, *Can't they see the teeth?* It bothers him that nobody else got this warning vibe, not even his old friend Ray Powell— retired lawyer, runs Kraventown from behind the scenes.

It bothers him that nobody else got that warning vibe, not even meticulous Ray. Ray takes his time making up his mind, just not that day. Ray, *his friend Ray* walked Steele into Merrill's office at Town Planning and Zoning and introduced them smooth as Judas, and Merrill drank the Kool-Aid too, which bothers him the most.

Then on Friday she took his hands the way she does, laughing. "Come on, sweetie. Ray's giving the party at Azalea House."

"For that guy."

"Is that a problem for you?"

He was cool about it, neither here or there. "Sorry, I have things to do."

They're too close to have to spell it out. She tried, "If you'd only *talk* to him. Really, he's in love with this place and so are you . . ." Then she read the sour look on his face and push almost came to shove; his smart, tough, longtime lover curled her fingers in the hollow at his throat, wheedling. "If you loved me, you'd come with."

He managed not to say, *Not in this life.* He tightened his hand over hers, keeping it in place, and did the best he could. "Tell Ray I'm sorry, tell him something came up."

Right. He should have gone, marked his territory, whatever men in love are supposed to do. Merrill came home glowing. "Davy, he can't figure out why you won't give him the time of day when he thinks you're doing great things here."

What???

"New buildings *and* renovations. What you did at the Lanier plantation, the big houses on Front Street, the Gaillard, for instance, the clinic. At least give him a chance!"

He loves her so he kept his mouth shut.

According to Ray, Rawson Steele worked that party like a pro. He'd played the genial, clueless tourist, *"Say, where's the best fishing, who makes the best crab cakes, are there any Civil War relics left on the island?"* translated: Confederate gold. He followed up with *"Who keeps up all these great old houses"* a beat too soon, Ray told him, which meant, *"Who are the first families?"* By the time the Japanese lanterns burned down and his guests were wandering off into the Carolina night, this aggressively charming intruder had his host backed into a corner. He was oblique, nothing stated, but all those questions narrowed down to: *"What would it take to buy these people out?"*

Davy said, "He looked like trouble coming in."

Ray, who'd planted torchères along the walks at Azalea House and fired up his champagne fountain in this guy's honor, finished, "Turns out you were right, Ribault. You. Were. Right."

Here in the low country, on the barrier islands along the Inland Waterway, on Kraven island in particular, people don't land on you like that. They don't expect you to unzip your fly at the first party and show them your junk. In these parts folks amble in, and if there's something on their mind they take their time getting around to it, idling until you ask.

Ray backed off that night and he wasn't the only one. In the low country, people do these things so smoothly that outsiders never know. Davy kept his distance, but every day he has coffee with the dawn patrol at Weisbuch's store, and he hears. They say Steele is here for something about their island— land, he thinks— which puts David A. Ribault of Ribault Associates, Architects, squarely in his sights, which is a problem for him. Davy isn't OCD exactly, but as a kid he fell in love with symmetry, and he became an architect because of the need to put things right. He'd like to take the jumbled mass of the town, all these decaying houses and ramshackle shanties and cheap new buildings badly designed, and find a way to improve them, daring to hope that will make things better for people living here, whereas this bastard, bastard . . . He doesn't know. But he does. *He wants to fuck up our island.* No. *He wants to fuck us up by messing with everything we care about.*

For days he and Steele circled each other like dogs deciding whether to fight or not. He'd just as soon they didn't, but when he slouched out of Weisbuch's early yesterday, Steele blindsided him. "Ribault!"

"Shit!" Bastard, bastard: hot coffee everywhere.

"We have to meet."

"Whatever happened to hello?"

Eyes narrowed: "Urgent matter."

"Say what?" Davy was not about to ask why. He wasn't about to say yes, either.

"We need to sit down." Steele was all Abe Lincoln forelock and disarming, trust-me grin, but those black eyes darted here, there. With a fake half-smile, he rushed on. "Not here, over there on the mainland, where it's . . ."

Fill in the blanks.

"It's . . ." Davy prompted, leaving Steele a space to put the rest, but Steele didn't. *What does he want from me?*

"How's tomorrow?"

Davy studied the lanky Northerner: dark hair, dark, deep-set eyes, really does look like Abraham Lincoln on a good day, except without the beard. *Would you trust this man?* Davy doesn't trust anybody much, except Merrill. And Ray, who yanked him out of Charlton Community College and drop-kicked him into New Haven to start all over again at Yale. "What for?"

Steele used the proffer: big man extends hand with generous grin to prove that he's bigger than you. "Rawson Steele." *Shake.*

"I know." Davy shook, sort of, in a classic feint-and-lunge. Two guys who don't like each other much, bent on faking each other out.

"We need a time certain."

"I need a reason."

Steele countered with the blow-off line of the century. "I'll explain later. Tomorrow?"

Davy wheeled. "Can't. Busy." Take *that* and fuck you.

"Wait!" Steele followed, matching him step for step. "This is . . ."

"What?" Davy snapped around in a full 360, glaring. "What!"

"It's . . ." This is when he got weird. "I don't want to cause a panic but this is serious, and you look like the right man . . ."

If I ask, he wins. Make him wait.

Steele waited a beat too long. He said, "Something's about to," and didn't finish. He said, "It's just." But he didn't say just what. He said what was a good place on the mainland, where they could meet out in the open, where no third party can plant a bug. As if granting a concession, he said, "Name the place."

Davy didn't. He just grinned. "No bugs?"

"You heard me."

Davy studied him: silk shirt, hundred-dollar jeans and four-hundred-dollar high-tops. Like he went into Barneys and said, "country" and this is what he got, never looked at the tags, just let them run his plastic, all condescending, thinking: *South Carolina? Hicks. This is good enough for them.*

Davy's grin spread. *Welcome to the boondocks, friend.* He held off answering until he had Steele gnawing the cuticles around his buffed fingernails. "Historic Charlton waterfront?"

"Someplace convenient to your office."

So you did break in, you condescending fuck. Like I'll take you into the back room and show you everything.

They faced off like captains of opposing teams, hicks versus assholes. "Outside, no bugs? Then you'll want the Front Street Overlook." Davy flashed his best hick grin.

Steele didn't bother to fake a smile. "Directions, please. I need to tell my phone."

Like any app could track the network of causeways and bridges linking the barrier islands to town. He really is not from around here. Pissed, he started before Steele hit **record**: "OK, Lewis Cooder bridge off Kraven, take Route Six across Poynter's island to the Calhoun bridge to the causeway. It's a straight shot to the Bartlett Fork. Now, look sharp and watch the signs or you'll end up at the base on North Island, apologizing to the MPs on the gate. Got that?"

As if. Steele was all thumbs. Grinning, Davy went on. "Your next turn's at the three-foot-tall milestone, you can't miss it, big block letters. Take a right and you're headed for Charlton." The milestone reads: RIBAULT ROAD. His family was in the first wave of Huguenots, so far back that people forget. "Charlton High's on your left, we used to. Never mind. Bear right at Pinckney Street. Big money built on the waterfront, it's all Tara and Belle Reve on the left, facing the bay. Look for the Overlook where the live-oaks thin out?"

"Wait!"

"Live-oaks, did you not Google us?" He was gratified to see Steele, all thwarted and fuming when all he has to do is get a damn map. Grinning, Davy dragged it out, "You know, all Spanish moss, like gorilla armpit hair? At the Tanner house, pull into the lot across the street."

He had Steel barking with frustration. "Tanner house?"

"Man, it's on all the damn posters! Civil War hospital. They rolled all the crippled Yankee soldiers out on the porch to watch the sun come up." Davy finished with his easy, trust-me grin.

He laid back for a minute, wanting Steele to process what he said next.

"You wanted a place that can't be bugged."

"Right. Privacy." Steele fixed Davy with those dead-black eyes. "You'll need it."

"Nope." Nobody tells Dave Ribault what he needs without it costing. Fool Yankee, with his No Bugs. *I'll show you bugs.*

Steele dropped the next words like bricks. "You don't know what you need."

Raising the possibility that after last night he and Merrill . . . *Don't, Ribault. Be cool.* "I'll be under the Charlton Oak, big tree, big plaque. You get one half-hour, tops." Then he walked right into it. "What time?"

Steele made a quick calculation: turned out it was get-even time. Given their schedules and whatever he has on his plate that he needs to keep private Steele said, "Early."

"How early?"

"At 4:30," the Northerner said with a *gotcha* grin. Then he drove in the last nail. "If you want everything you care about to be where you left it when you get home tomorrow . . ." he said, but did not finish. Son of a bitch walked away whistling through his teeth like Davy ought to know the tune and pick up on the words, but, shit.

He went to work pissed off, and drew and redrew a site plan because he couldn't make it come out *right.* It made him late getting back to Merrill's house so he stayed pissed off, and when he rolled into the driveway, his bad day personified was standing with Merrill at her front door, two heads bent under the yellow porch light. Close. Like they were colluding.

It's not that she's Davy's private property, but they are, by God, *together,* everybody knows that. He got out of the car locked and loaded, but by the time he crunched through the azaleas Merrill was inside and Steele was gone. He didn't ask and she didn't say, they just sat down to a late supper in front of the TV so nobody had to talk, but it ate him out like a mess of chiggers, burrowing under the skin. He'd do anything to make it stop: pace, eat, confront her, but he didn't know what.

They collided in her kitchen in the middle of the night and faced off like gladiators— why?

He thinks he snarled, *What was that with you and Rawson Steele?* and they had words. She cried, *That's what I'm trying to find out,* which should have diffused it— if he'd just let it go, but he couldn't, so push came to shove the way it does with them: her strong mind, his will. By the end he was raging, *Dammit, I moved all the way out here just to be with you* and Merrill said if that's the way he felt about it, he should damn well put up or shut up and God help him, he doesn't know which. It was stone dark when he slipped out of bed today with all that between them, and nothing resolved. He could care less whether Steele's stupid meeting comes off, but the fight stuck to his hide like a burr under a saddle and rubbed him raw. OK, he fled the scene of the crime. He left Kraven island long before Boogie Hood shuffled out of the back room to start the coffee, raised the Rolos and turned on the light in front of Weisbuch's store.

Now

Driving to town in the dark, he broods. Why this frontal assault on Kraven island, and his girl Merrill in particular? What, exactly, is driving Rawson Steele?

It's so early that no birds fly. The only sign of life in the sky above the Inland Waterway is a transport plane taking off from the base at North Island. Even the bugs seething in the marsh grass along the causeways are still. He should have but didn't leave some kind of note for Merrill, she won't mind, they don't take each other for granted, they're not on that kind of footing, but after last night . . . At the end it got ugly, both of them hurt and angry, tearing up the night.

Oh shit. *Oh, shit.*

Anger twists in his belly like a mess of gators seething in the marsh. He wrenches the car off the road at the Overlook and pulls into the parking lot. Four A.M. Good. He's first. Fine. Go out on the breakwater and watch the morning come up. Make the bastard wait. From the breakwater, he'll see Steele's car coming before the fool figures out where to park. Given the lay of the land, he'll have to stand up with a big, hick wave before Steele even knows that his mark or his quarry, nemesis or whatever, got here first.

Davy will write his first line based on the look of Steele as he approaches, gauge his intentions by the way he walks. See if he gassed up that Lexus or hotwired another car. Make him wait until he's gnawed his fingers raw, and make him wait some more. If he so much as looks like he's fixing to leave, keep him in place with one phone call: "Bridge is up, be there soon." String it out, Ribault. String it out. Eventually his mark will get sick of pacing and sit down under the famous Charlton Oak. Being as he's not from around here, he'll lean against that big, speckled trunk and start messing with his smartphone, Davy thinks, everybody does.

That's when I drop down to the fisherman's ledge and come back around on him, so it looks like I just drove in. He'll give Steele his patented sweet, apologetic grin, show his empty hands and go, "Hey. Don't get up." By that time the Northerner's pants will be alive with redbugs: chiggers gnawing through his thong or burrowing deep inside the butt-crack of those high-end jeans. At this or any other hour the little fuckers snap to and swarm out of the bark or up from the Spanish moss the second they smell fresh meat.

It's a pleasure to think about them having whatever urgent conversation Steele planned while he's all distracted and crazy because he can't let Merrill Poulnot's lover, her *partner* see him scratching his butt.

There is a shift in the air— an atmospheric tremor, as though something tremendous just stirred and came to life, but he is too angry to mark the difference.

Whatever was about to happen just happened, but Davy doesn't know it yet.

Instead, his heart is running on ahead. He has to get done here and rush home before Merrill even thinks about waking up. He has to make things right. The more Davy mulls it, the more he thinks her ultimatum is directly caused by this fucking Steele, an observation he is too messed up to parse. Where is the fucker, anyway? If it gets to be five A.M. and he hasn't showed, the hell with him. They're done. He'll wait until the last trawler passes, guys he knew in high school fixing to cast their nets out there just like their fathers did. When he studied architecture and set up shop on Charlton Street, he had great dreams. Instead it's a constant tug-of-war between his vision and predators like Steele, and if he envies the shrimpers a little bit? Well, yeah. So cool, spending your days out on the open water, nothing to think about; cast the nets and drift until sunset, haul in your catch.

Fuck Steele, with his "I'll explain later." The light is changing and he has things to do. Get home, take Merrill by the hands and not let go until they've ended this, he tells himself, without knowing what *this* is.

Then sirens tear up the sunrise, the blat and confusion of some new emergency. Warning? *Warning.*

Trouble out there somewhere.

He is up and running too fast for thought to catch up, shaken, worried and wondering.

Where?

2

Merrill Poulnot
Yesterday morning

Nobody saw this coming.

Waking up in our usual lives on Kraven island yesterday, who knew? Lying there with Davy, doing everything we loved to do, I didn't have a clue. When we're linked, we're one body; when we're apart, we're like twins separated at birth— if one of us is hurt, the other flinches, but now . . .

Who knew? How could anybody know?

Look at us the way we were, lounging in the sweet morning air, lazy islanders getting up to go about our business: Davy and me lying close, the hundred other souls stirring around us hitting the snooze alarm, putting off the usual things— making coffee, putting out the dog. We were so *ordinary*.

Yesterday.

Yesterday I was troubled by certain things, but nothing that hasn't worried me every day since I moved out on Father and left my little brother there with him. *Ned won't have the same problem,* I told myself; *boys don't,* but I felt shitty about it. He was only six. I put sweet old Patrice in place to make sure of it, she was with us before Neddy was born, before Mother left us in the middle of the night. I ran away to save my life. I had to separate, rent a room and find a job, get into college— with funding— and come back strong enough to turn three lives around. I started with mine.

"Patrice will take care of you." I gave Neddy a phone. I showed him how to use it, walked him through a list of things to do in case of this, in case of that, thinking, *Thank God he's not a girl.* He was so grown up, reciting the list, all smart and proud. I promised to come see him every day, and I did. *Patrice will know what happens before it happens,* I told myself; *Patrice will take care of him,* and she did, and I checked on them daily. I went to junior college in Charlton so I could get back to the house every night, and by the time I went to State, Ned was tough enough to handle Father— and we had Patrice. We talked every night. On the phone with people you love, you can tell whether they're lying or not. It's in that vibe, or hesitation: some offbeat note in the voice.

Neddy doesn't lie, and Patrice can't. Every time I came home I looked for evidence: *One mark on my kid brother and I come down on him with the full force of the law.* I thought, *Child Services.* I thought, *The courts won't care who Father is or who his people were, when I graduate, Neddy will come to live with me.* I thought once I had the job, got this house, the court would let Ned decide, but I was wrong. I'm too young, I'm living with a man, we're not married, bad influence. QED. Meanwhile Father's at Trinity every Sunday, front row, kneeling on the spot where the first Poulnots knelt down to pray: solid citizen, the last in a long, long line of Hampton Poulnots. Until he stepped down for reasons he won't talk about, he was a judge.

I love my brother, but given what came down after Mother left, I can't be there at night. Instead I go every day, assess the situation. Make mental notes, one of those things I can't tell Davy about, or won't, *never let the people hear you grind your teeth.* Yesterday I found Father at the kitchen table with his

TELL IT TO THE JUDGE coffee mug and his oatmeal, everyday Father, making the smile he uses when he knows he is being watched, sweet old man, wouldn't hurt a fly.

"Where's Neddy?"

He looks up: *Oh, it's you.* "What?"

Things have always been bad between us. "Ned. You know, Edward Poulnot, your only son?"

"At that damn computer, he's always at that damn confuser— I mean computer. If he's playing those games I'll go up and . . ."

"Don't."

The rest of the sentence goes: *Tan his hide.* My father, the retired judge, leader of men, back-benched at town meetings, contains the rage, but I know.

"Just don't."

Blink. Blink. "I wouldn't think of it." Pillar of the community, butter wouldn't melt, sweet old Father, mild as milk. Fine old family, solid citizen— that's what most people think; they'd rather not know. He needs the applause.

And what did I need? I needed to go upstairs and speed-read my brother's face, looking for bruises; ruffle his hair, checking his head for lumps. I needed to look into his face and without waiting for the answer, find out from Ned without having to ask, *Are you all right?* It hasn't happened yet, but I worry. All these years and it's still precarious. Patrice is embarrassed by the extra money, but she understands, and she knows why I can't be there. Grandmother left me a little so I can afford to do this— did she know before I knew? Father drove me away with his drunken rages, the night crawlers: Father in my room; I was never sure what, or why. *Ned's fine,* I told myself. *He's a boy.* He'll be fourteen next month, and he's already big enough to hit back.

"I'll just run upstairs and tell him hey."

I found him staring into the magic box. I know what Ned is looking for: power, and in the game, he's deep into it, scheming, slashing and blasting his way to the top level of that gorgeous CG mountain. He didn't even hear me come in.

I began, just the way I always do. "Are you OK?"

Then I watched reflected fires and explosions playing on his face. He said, without looking up, "I'm fine."

Ned, Edward LaMar Poulnot, you look so much like our mother that it breaks my heart, sitting there mousing and grinning as the neon blood flies, lighting you up and filling your world here, and inside that game. I know you have something going with your friends in there; I know you talk to them in the night, tapping into the chat box with one hand while you mouse deeper and deeper into the game, the game! I was a gamer once; I know it doesn't matter which game it is, when you're into it, that's all you are. It swallows you whole, and if I watch for more than a minute or two I'll get sucked in and there will be two of us sitting here, lost in space and it will be wonderful, at least for a little while.

"Don't you have school?"

"Home sick."

"You look fine to me."

"Sore throat. Sent home yesterday, in case. If my tongue turns red around the edges, it's strep." The magic box makes that **kphchuuu** sound better than kids do, and on the screen, whatever he is fighting dies. "Got a note from the nurse."

"Show me."

"Can't, I'll miss the . . ." **Kphchuuu!**

"If you say so. If you're not up and around when I get here tomorrow, we're going to the clinic on Poynter, so Dr. LaPointe can culture your throat, you hear?"

KPHU, SKLZZT. FOW! A flying reptile thing swoops down on his character. "I *said,* do you hear?"

That thing is poised to destroy you. Neddy, watch out!

BLAT!!

Oh, thank God. "Earth to Ned." Late. *There's a hidden button on that sword. If he can only find that red button in the hilt* . . . One more minute and I'd be late.

"OK."

"Sick, huh." *Oh look, stairs up to a— temple? Neddy, watch out for the* . . . I have to go. "Call me if you get worse. Say hi to Patrice for me."

BRAAAACK . . . Sweet grin as he waves. "Later, dude."

It was a relief to get to work, where I know what to do and how to do it and my check comes on the last Friday of the month.

Then at the end of the day the gorgeous stranger I met through Ray Powell showed up at my front door—Ray's friend—at least I think he is—Rawson Steele. I looked into his face and I thought, *Ray, we need to talk.* Rawson tried to smile for me but his face wouldn't hold still. The lines changed like crystals in a kaleidoscope, so fast that I couldn't read anything but this: he needed me. It was mysterious. Intense. His voice escaped him almost by accident. "There's something I have to find out, it's . . ."

It was interesting, Rawson Steele all urgent and vulnerable. Here. I touched his arm. There was a little electric shock as we connected, a current so strong that I had to ask, "Are you all right?"

"Ms. Poulnot." He began, but couldn't quite get it out: *this is so hard.* "Merrill, there's something I have to . . ."

Davy roared into our driveway just then and broke the connection. He banged on the horn at the sight of us, cutting an angle so sharp that oyster shells sprayed like spit, and when I turned back to Rawson Steele to ask him what he needed from me, or why, he wasn't anywhere.

By the time Davy came into the house it was like the stranger was something I had imagined. Davy didn't kiss me, he just set his jaw and went all stony, so I knew it was real. He stood there waiting for me to explain. He'd rather die than ask, but he wouldn't let go. We sat down to eat angry, watched TV angry, turning up the volume to avert the confrontation. We went to bed angry, couldn't sleep. Got up and had the fight, and whose fault was that?

I was too upset to lie awake feeling bad about it which I did— feel bad, I mean. Last night I didn't care what Davy said or did to make up, I was that pissed off, so I took a damn pill. If he tried to apologize I wouldn't know it. If we turned over in the morning and rolled together the way we usually do— well, I couldn't think about that. Not the way I was. I clamped my pillow over my head and around my ears to shut him out, and I felt good about it. Cut off from Davy, snug and drowsy in the dark.

Until, without warning and with no sense of transition . . .

This.

3

Davy
Thursday

Two cop cars and an ambulance stream past, heading out Ribault Road. Trouble on the base, he thinks. There's always trouble at the base. On North Island the front and back ends of war rub up against each other and strike sparks daily, old vets and new war wounded laid up in the base hospital while buzz-cut eighteen-year-olds train to feed the war, result: bar fights and domestic violence. Losses on night marches—AWOL via the marsh.

Then a procession of EMTs and fire trucks makes the V-turn, heading out Ribault Road. *This is bigger than I thought.* Davy checks his phone; after five, and no Steele. History tells him that even at this hour, any kind of commotion on the base jams up traffic at the Bartlett Fork. *Five more minutes,* he tells himself. *If he made it around the Fork he'll be here by then.*

Police set up a checkpoint as he watches, waving island-bound traffic to the old Burton road. Dude, you can get there from here but it takes hours. Right. They're already backed up bumper to bumper from here to the county's built-in bottleneck, the circle at the Bartlett Fork.

He'll have to wait until the cops step aside and traffic actually moves. With things the way they are, it could eat up the rest of the morning.

Just when he has to get home.

Fucking Steele. *What did he want with me?*

Home. *Why isn't he here?*

Home invasion by Rawson Steele. *Why was he on my porch last night, standing too close to my girl?*

The porch is Merrill's, but they've been together for so long that he forgets. With no sign of Steele and whatever hangs between the two of them still pending, Davy goes back inside his head and broods. She has to see through this guy, right? Walking in with sharp elbows and that loaded smile, who would not? In the South, you're brought up to be polite, smile for the stranger, at least until he shows himself for what he really is.

Whatever that is. Davy groans.

Does Steele want something that we don't know about? Oil beneath the surface of Kraven island? Confederate gold buried under the Tanner house or in trunks at the bottom of the lake? Pirate treasure in a drowned ship out there beyond the sand bar on the ocean side? Treasure hunters have dug all over the island and sent divers down into those waters for going on two hundred years, and the most anybody ever found was Earl Pinckney's Spanish piece of eight, and that washed up on the beach when they were ten. Maybe the island is hiding some great natural resource that we don't know about; turn our backs and he'll leach it out of the ground, bleed us dry without us knowing until it's gone.

Or he's a developer, all charming at first, vampire just waiting for you to invite him in. He'll buy out the homefolks one by one and level the island to do . . . what? Desecrate the place?

Will it be condos or plastic pseudo plantation houses with vinyl columns on the verandas and fake flowers in PermaStone urns? Great big honking casino, more likely. Megamall, harbor expansion that takes out our waterfront, so giant cruise ships can unload tourists to trash the island, some damn thing to wreck our lives and ruin the terrain, like a . . .

Davy is— Oh shit, he's circling the drain.

Like he could win me over before the sun comes up. Does he not know what I do for a living?

That's the bad thing about meeting: "Someplace convenient to your office." Yeah. He does.

If he thinks I'll cough up deeds and property lines just because he asks, he's shit out of luck. I'll kill him first.

The problem being that Davy isn't sure. Steele is like a Chinese puzzle— you can't solve it, and you can't let it go. His mind is whirring like a rat trapped in a gerbil wheel.

Wait! While he was brooding, the pink light in the sky turned blue. It's late! He needs to hurl himself at that traffic jam and hope to God that he gets home before Merrill signs off on him.

It takes some fancy dancing to make it through the second check point at Ribault Road, but Davy manages. He went through Charlton Primary with most of these guys. He's making decent headway when sirens pull him over: with Charlton cops already out there, fire trucks and emergency vehicles from towns surrounding stream past him, headed for the Bartlett Fork. *Trouble at the base,* he thinks. *Really bad trouble at the base.*

He's moving an inch at a time, banging on his car radio because for whatever reasons, reception is totally whacked. Every few minutes another gang of sirens pulls everybody over while more cop cars, fire trucks, wreckers, ambulances pass. Traffic seizes up altogether a crazy half-mile short of the circle. *Not now. Not when I'm so close!* A good half-mile of outgoing cars clogs the road between here and the circle, more are piling up behind him and the sun is high.

He should call or text Merrill, but the signal is crunchy and he doesn't know what to say. *Bad idea. Wait. I'd better talk to her;* he hits One on his speed-dial, and his phone? His service makes calls from the causeway dicey on the best days. Now the signal is all fucked up. *What, did lightning take out the phone towers?* He needs to fix what he wrecked, and he can't do it by phone. He needs to look into those hazel eyes and try to guess what she's thinking, what he has to do, he . . .

Doesn't know.

Anybody with half a brain would do what people behind him are doing: crunch over the median divider in a complete U-turn, incoming traffic from the islands or no, and head back to town. Makes sense, the morning's shot, but he can't. He's too in love, or driven, or whatever it is, to quit now. It's all he can think about. Dumb, sticking wallpaper music into his CD deck, like that would take his mind off the fact that nothing is moving and for the moment, there's no place to go.

How long has he been sitting here? Another half-hour, and nothing's moved. Crazy, stupid, stupid-crazy Dave Ribault, waiting like a toad. It's time to charge the median, make that Uey and head back to town, where he can make this call from a land-line, no interference breaking up the important things they have to say. He guns the motor. Wait.

This is bad.

There is no incoming traffic.

Not one car or truck has come in from the barrier islands— no military personnel or official vehicles coming back from whatever disaster at the base.

The car in front of him jerks to life and Davy's heart fast-forwards. *At last.* Clinch, reconciliation, and then . . .

Then he rounds the last bend.

The causeway to North Island is all but empty. The trouble isn't on the base. It's out their way, maybe on Poynter's island, or, *my God! Kraven*. Davy's jaw seizes up. His teeth collide with a padlock *click*. He tries the car radio again but gets nothing but white noise.

Five more minutes and all his joints will rust. Time crawls. His car crawls. The skin on the back of his neck crawls. Ahead, orange cones and yellow plastic barrels mark a checkpoint, OK, SOP. Usually checkpoints are manned by guys like the ones he charmed his way past in town; if it's Bobie or Jack Stankey, he'll go, "Hey," and they'll go, "Well, hey." All he has to do is grin, hark them back to something they did after the Moultrie game in senior year and they'll flag him through. But this is a military operation: four Humvees from the base crouch with shoulders hunched, filling the road.

Roadblock, here at the bottleneck, and it's . . . He checks his watch. It's well past noon.

This is really bad.

MPs with handhelds and clipboards stand next to the military Humvees, grilling drivers of outgoing cars, checking licenses and registrations, car by car. They work in pairs, peering into backseats, popping every trunk. Other MPs are stationed around the circle, flagging cars onto this exit or that. They're diverting most drivers onto the dirt road through the Bartlett woods. It takes you back to downtown Charlton, but not anytime soon, and the rest? From the looks of it, only a few cars make it onto the causeway home. Certified islanders, Davy thinks, and he's not sure how this will play out. Although he was born in Charlton, he didn't move out to Kraven until Merrill loved him well enough. Now they live together in the little clapboard house on Poulnot Street. Look, Officer, it's been five years. He's done some of his best work on Kraven island so, is he a certified islander or not?

"Dave Ribault, from Kraven island. What's going on?"

"License and registration, sir. Please."

"The— whatever happened." He hands them over. "Is it on Poynter or on Kraven?"

"Only documented residents . . ."

"Dave Ribault, it's right there on the license. My people were . . ."

"I don't care what your people were."

"What's going on?"

MP Number One hands them back. "We're not authorized . . ."

"I have a . . ." He starts to say girlfriend, but it comes out, "I have a wife out there!" As he does so, two TV8 trucks rumble past and he thinks, *This is really bad.*

Number Two notes something on his clipboard.

Overhead, helicopters rattle the sky. *It's even worse than I thought.* Crazy, listening to his voice zigzagging. "Just tell me. What the hell is going on!"

The first MP hands back his paperwork. "Proceed."

As he flags Davy toward the channel bridge, Number Two's voice breaks just enough to let the truth leak out. "Nobody knows."

Naturally the drawbridge is up. He tries the phone again; he's stopped caring what they say to each other, he needs to know she's OK. There's crap reception out here even on a good day, which this is not. He dies a dozen times, squirming until the drawbridge closes and he and the few cars backed up behind him go across to Poynter's island.

The main drag in Poyntertown is packed solid with cars and pissed-off drivers trying to get somewhere. Given the lay of the land, it's expected. As a kid, he came out here to Earl's house so often that he knows the island by heart. Anybody who's been crabbing in the swash knows there's another way to the Kraventown causeway. Never mind that it's longer, and there are wet patches that you have to ford and places you can bog down, depending on the tides. It beats stasis, which is what this is.

He peels off and heads for the beach road. The crushed oyster shells will rip the hell out of his tires and that's the least of it, but he doesn't care. He'll be at the Kraven island ON ramp and on the causeway before those poor suckers jammed up in Poyntertown figure out that in terms of forward motion, they're screwed.

Making his way around the island, he plans. Merrill left for work hours ago, so he'd better think up a terrific explanation for him leaving without stopping to kiss her goodbye and make up for whatever that was that fell between them last night. *Think, asshole, it had better be damn good.* He needs to pick up something at Weisbuch's— wait. A late lunch won't make up for what they said to each other. No way. He needs to drop into Fowler's Gems on Bay Street and find her something terrific, grin like he drove all the way in to Charlton before dawn looking for this essential pretty Thing, wasted the morning shopping in town and got hung up in the monster traffic jam. He'll play up the trouble he went to, trashing his undercarriage on the oyster shells, throwing palm fronds into the road to keep from sinking into the sludge, *and guess what, all that time wasted and your present was right here, in the front window of Fowler's jewelry store.*

Who cares what it costs, he owes her. Tennis bracelet, he thinks, linked baby diamonds, because until they make up for things they said to each other. Wait. Given the last thing she said to him. Well, a diamond ring might be cheaper, but it would be all wrong. *Wrong,* he thinks, rounding the last bend, uneasy and distracted. *Wrong,* he tells himself, trying out and discarding a dozen possible right things to say.

Everything I said and did last night was wrong. I have to make it better, I have to do this right, I . . .

Never thought the trouble that brought half the rolling stock in South Carolina to these islands was at home.

Holy crap!

The Kraventown causeway ramp is blocked. Yellow plastic barrels bar the ON ramp. Beyond them, yellow tape protects the police vehicles lined up across the causeway, closing off all four lanes. Uniformed personnel guard the barricades, while others lug in sawhorses stenciled POLICE LINE— DO NOT CROSS to keep back the growing crowd. Angry islanders and frustrated commuters tangle, running up each other's heels.

Compared to this, the mess at Bartlett Circle looked like the Azalea Ball. Uniformed personnel stand on the raised causeway between here and the Kraven island bridge.

The cops and troopers marshaled on the causeway look to be at a loss. The ones on the bridge beyond are at the rail, peering into the dark waters like they expect to see something down there that they don't know about. Others are bent double, looking under cars that look like they got caught in some storm and froze solid in mid-crossing. Every vehicle he can see is dead empty, and this bothers Davy for reasons he doesn't want to think about.

If the drivers bailed for some reason after they left Kraventown, where did they go? More than a dozen dead cars sit up there on the causeway like gulls on a wire strung between here and home.

Davy noses his Wrangler up the grade to the row of barrels blocking the ON ramp and gets out, thinking to walk around the markers and find somebody to tell him what came down out there, but they're all busy, frantic with it, whatever it is.

He shouts, to everybody in general. "What's going on?"

An angry voice he can't source shouts back, "Don't know. Nobody does."

Cleverly, Davy rolls a barrel aside, jiggling it until there's a gap big enough to slip through. He needs to stand face to face with somebody who does. A state trooper intercepts him. "Back off. Nobody on the causeway past this point."

He presses forward. "I live over there!"

"So do a lot of folks, Mister." Davy thinks he said, "Or they did."

"What happened, what the fuck happened?"

"Too soon to tell."

"But my . . ." *whole life is over there.*

"No civilians allowed."

"I have to see my . . ."

"You have to go."

The trooper doesn't exactly aim his weapon at Davy, just nudges him back with it, nosing the barrel higher and higher, stampeding Davy toward the crowd crammed behind the police tape. He can either scramble up the bank and join the gawkers or get back in his car, take off the brakes and roll backward down the ramp and go back the way he came, aware as he does so that there are places he will have to ford and places where he may get stuck in the shifting sand.

Back. No way is he going back.

Davy fake-leaves the ramp, moon-walking backward until the trooper is satisfied and turns away. At this point, it seems important to study uniforms, find somebody he knows. "Hey, Jack," he shouts. They've known each other since first grade. "Jack Stankey."

The Poyntertown cop turns. "Yo."

"What the fuck happened?"

"I'm not authorized to say." Exact same speech the MPs back

at the Bartlett Circle recited. Jack's face is empty, a surface that was just wiped clean.

Someone shouts, "He doesn't fucking know!"

"Nobody knows!"

Davy made it through the long morning on the belief that whatever happened was happening somewhere else; he's made it this far on the strength of a lie buzzing like a mantra inside of his head, *she's fine, nothing is wrong,* but with the sun high and the causeway deserted and the unknown at work on Kraven island, with no way to find out what's going on out there and no access, everything is wrong. "What?" he cries. "What!"

A high, clear voice knifes through the confusion, cutting deep. "They're all gone."

Desperate to source it, Davy whirls. "What?"

"Gone," she cries.

He looks here, there. *"What!"*

"They all vanished. Every mortal soul on Kraven is gone!"

4

Merrill Poulnot
The first day

. . . This.

This what? What! In the void Father roars, "This is outrageous," and for a second I'm seventeen again and living at home, trapped on that runaway express train to despair.

This nightmare! I grope for Davy, but my hand closes on a foreign body and I snap awake. For a strangled second, Delroy Root grabs hold and we hug, but our bodies know better and we recoil— nothing personal, just, *ewww*: *not-Davy*.

Delroy, grieving and baffled: *not-Ada*. Blinded by the glare, we lock hands and cling.

Blink.

Poleaxed, he and I let go. I lunge here, there in the sudden, staggering heat, blinded by sun glinting off the dead white buildings that surround us like slabs of porcelain waiting to be toppled.

There are at least a hundred of us here. One second we were safe in our houses, submerged in the last sleep before the alarm or just starting the day— steam on the bathroom mirror from the shower, coffee brewing, morning eggs on the stove; we were still in bed, some of us, half-awake and fumbling for early-morning sex. I was stone sleeping while the others nodded over breakfast or got the jump on commuter traffic to the mainland two bridges and one island away from Kraven island.

Between heartbeats, we were picked up and— what— *transported*.

We came as we were, in whatever we slept in or put on to face the day, a hundred thunderstruck citizens of Kraven island, set down in the middle of nothing. We don't know how it happened or what happened. We were all happily doing whatever we did every morning on Kraven island, hitting the snooze alarm, walking the dog or bringing in the morning paper, texting or skimming the Web, ordinary people sleepwalking through the moment, not thinking about what our lives would be like if all this luxury that we took for granted, ended.

Then without transition, we were here.

Missing? Me? Why a minute ago I was . . .

Sand gusts into the bleak enclosure where we— fell? Landed in this compound, enclave, porcelain basin set down in a desert, contained in this glossy, bleached out— what?

What is this place?

Dropped into a square of gleaming, featureless buildings in a dead desert town where nothing grows, shaken and muttering, most of us, we try to locate ourselves, while at the periphery of the plaza where we landed, Father bellows, bloated with rage. Mother woke me with tears in her eyes the night she fled him. "Look after your baby brother," she said and I have, until— where is he? *Oh God, oh, God!*

"Ned, do you hear me? Neddy! Ned! Edward Lamar Poulnot, you stand up and signify!" It's so crowded that I can't make him out. Whirling under the bleached sky, I fix on the flagpole, standing tall in the middle of this mob. There's no flag at the top to identify this place or tell us what country we're in or

whether it's a country at all, just a windsock flapping, loose ropes
rattling against the shaft.

"Ned Poulnot, do you hear?" Together, we shuffle and fret
under the murderous sun, miserable and confused, struggling
to orient ourselves, to comprehend, while Father runs around
the margins with his knees going, like pistons on a broken machine, battering the universe with that big, ugly voice.

"Ned?" If I can only find Ned, then I know I'll find Davy. I'll
find him and. Then what? "Davy! Dave! Has anybody seen Dave
Ribault?"

But all I hear back is Father, raging like Moses with the tab-
lets raised, ready to smash them on the cement in the plaza of
this weird, dead town. Then *people I thought I knew* fix on the
one thing they recognize in the confusion and turn to Father for
orders, forgetting the drunken rages and how that usually
ends.

Thank God, Ray Powell cuts him off at the pass. My excellent
friend and the real power behind Kraventown; he's famous for his
soft touch. They don't know it, but Ray keeps even the worst of
us in check. Last year he removed Father from the bench so
smoothly that the town thought he was retiring to write the history of the Poulnots, three centuries' worth. While the rest of us
were flailing, Ray's been scouting the plaza— the glistening surfaces of the buildings that dominate on four sides. Four exits: four
diagonal roads that lead out of the square, and at its center, the
flagpole. Mounting the marble steps to the top of the pedestal,
Ray has found the highest point in this place, a square apparently
designed to level or subdue anyone who enters here.

Standing tall, Ray shouts, "Over here," and everyone in the
plaza turns to him, all at once, leaving Father to rail on, forgotten.

"This way!" Ray lifts us with his voice and turns us around in that easy, commanding way he has. "Fresh clothes!"

Furious, Father rants while the rest of us, undressed or half-dressed, gather around the bin on the cement at the base of the flagpole where Ray stands. Subdued and gasping, we slip on scrubs to cover ourselves. Flip-flops for the ones transported without shoes and hopping from foot to foot on the hot cement.

We were expected.

This was.

White scrubs. Like costumes, but for what? Shakespeare in the plaza or electroshock in some occult institution? The rectangle of white façades in the plaza looks fake, like the set for an opera that got too ambitious for any stage— which raises the question. If we are in some kind of production, what's it about? Was it written for us? Why are we here?

Then Father, *my father,* mounts the base to the flagpole and throws himself at the ropes, trying to stand higher than Ray. He scrambles on up the pole, hand-over-hand until his strength fails. In the seconds before Ray catches him, he bawls: *"Why are you doing this to us?"*

Which begs the real questions. Where are we, anyway? Why?

As it turns out, those aren't the real questions either, but we don't know that. All we know is that we're the world's greatest mystery, and we know this— how?

Color blazes. On the biggest façade in the plaza, a great screen blooms like a tropical flower. We're on TV! As though the Power, whatever it is, whatever they are— as though some mysterious entity heard my old man howling and flipped a switch.

We stop what we were saying, doing, thinking, and face the screen like recruits lined up for the orientation film:

Welcome to Wherever This Is.

Wedged into the square like illegals waiting to be deported, we watch, waiting for the emcee, director, instructor, captors, the power behind our *removal* to step out and explain.

Instead, the show begins. *Island Inhabitants Vanish*. Long shot of Kraven island. A banner zips across the bottom of the screen on a loop: **Weekly World News**. My heart lifts. *We're on the news. This means they'll find us soon.*

But there's a problem. The travelogue-perfect montage is too detailed to be shot and edited in a day, the interviews so slick that questions stir in my gut, gnawing their way out. No power could have processed all that material in the short time we've been gone, but like everybody else watching, I was mesmerized. Changed. For that moment, in the aftermath of our— disruption and *removal,* I bought it. We all did.

Even Father goes quiet, fixed on the screen, but I know what he is thinking, standing there with his hands spread and his angry mouth ajar: civic leader, waiting for his cameo, while I speed-read the images; if Davy isn't here, I'll find him up there on the screen and find a way to let him know I'm here.

Cameras pan the route from Charlton to Poynter's island to our island. God, they've barricaded the causeway! It's so weird, all those driverless cars stalled on the road out of Kraventown; I don't see Davy's, so, *where!* Bay Street is so *still* that even Ray groans. Buildings we go into every day stand empty; shops and guest houses, even the police station, clinic, the banks. All our favorite and our private places are laid open like corpses waiting to be autopsied, doors sagging like empty mouths and all our secret orifices gaping.

On streets where we used to play, nothing moves but a stray cat slinking across the road with its ass tucked under in shame. Although we have audio there's no sound on Kraven, really, except for Wade Tanner's watchdogs snarling as the camera passes his jewelry store. It's so quiet that even at that great, unspecified distance, I hear marsh beetles crackling in the sawgrass off Ray Powell's dock. Then a news anchor reaches into one of the abandoned cars on the causeway and honks the horn, and all our dogs begin barking at once.

In case we thought we were deluded or dreaming, a great late-breaking news banner replaces **World News**. Racing along below the feed, our situation in précis:

THE KRAVEN ISLAND MYSTERY
Authorities Baffled— A Hundred Gone

Information comes thick and fast: news clips of baffled authorities' press conferences, interviews with mystified friends and strangers from the mainland and the outer islands, some of them in tears— *they're out there looking. Davy too?*

Then parents and friends and lovers of the missing— us!— plead with kidnappers, in case— *wait! is this a ransom situation?*— offering millions if whoever has us lets us go. In extreme closeup, the governor of South Carolina reports that the military, state police, local cops, supernumeraries, firefighters from three counties are blanketing the area. With an election coming up, he weeps. "And the sickening thing about this is that we've scoured the town and surrounding farmland, walked the perimeter of the island and dredged the channel and no living person is left behind on Kraven island to tell the tale." *Drama queen.*

"Our men found food cooking on the stove in some of those houses. Their pillows were still warm!"

Cut to Miss Edna Massingale, Crocker County historian. "It's as if they vanished from the face of the earth."

In the minutes— days?

This is when I begin to wonder.

In the weeks?

In the unspecified *time* since our mysterious disappearance, our houses look the same: no broken glass or shattered door-frames, no excavations or bullet holes, no signs of violence like bodies or crude barricades, nothing to suggest that we'd made a valiant last stand before we vanished or fled or were forcibly removed.

How long have we been here?

The mayor of Charlton has the nerve to wonder if we were seized by mass hysteria, running ahead of natural disaster, or plague? He looks concerned, but, God!

Viewers! What if there really is an epidemic? What if it threatened you, out there watching in your safe houses, snug among your pillows and panting for more? Bent on reassuring you, he blathers on, when all we want to know is that you're looking for us.

Worse. On our first day in this unknown, unknowable location, nobody knows, but everybody has a theory. Experts speculate at length, talking heads, huge and impotent, blathering on. Geologists, anthropologists, sociologists, show up on the giant screen; historians with graphs, sociologists with pie charts have opinions; officials and bounty hunters, mercenaries and earnest mainlanders air their views. A furious merchant claims we ran out on thousands in bad debts.

Asshole, we were *stolen*.

Meanwhile, even though Ray's holding him down, Father— my father!— comes to a boil. I should have seen it coming but I'm crazy with looking for Davy down here in the plaza and up there on the screen, and Davy isn't anywhere.

Cameras compound our grief by picking up details specific to us. They've been inside our houses— Father's cluttered kitchen, filthy dishes in the sink and in his bedroom, dirty clothes strewn on the floor. Close shot of his bedside table, that tin can with the fork standing upright in the baked beans. *What happened, Neddy. What happened to Patrice?* Shock cuts take us from Ray's sprawling, beautiful Azalea House to Kara Maxwell's cottage to the shack where Betsy Till and I played every day, wait, is this a documentary? Then . . .

My teeth lock. Close shot of the bed where I growled goodnight to Davy, not knowing it was goodbye. The bastard, bastards dished out a long closeup of our bedroom, where my lover got up in the dark and without an explanation, left.

It's all up close and so personal that it reams me out, and I'm not the only one, people all around me struggle, anxious and twitching with distress. It's all wrong, looking into the past we were yanked out of . . . how long ago?

Back when we had lives, and that's the issue.

Nobody could collect and edit that much data on a whole town in half a day. You couldn't video our island, interiors or exteriors, without somebody walking into the shot, so when did they . . .

Ray shouts, "What? What is this?" I turn to him for reassurance, the way you do, but something is off. I have to look again. Fully dressed as he is— khakis, nice shirt, starched explorer's vest with many pockets, he would have showered and shaved when he got up just like he did every morning, but. Some time today, while I was distracted and crazy with dislocation, Ray's freshly ironed clothes went to hell; my nails were white above the cuticles and we who shower every morning smell rank and unwashed, so the question isn't, where are we?

It's:

When?

5

Ned Poulnot

'Od damn, 'od damn, 'od damndamndammit, I'm deep into Level 299 of *Gaijin Samurai,* we are close to the top when the unexpected **awful** comes, and it's all been awful ever since. Like a shit bomb exploded my life, like, zot! No warning, no Take That, to let you know the looming nasty is coming, not even a threatening shadow or a flash of yellow eyes. It just smashes all over you in a great white wave, and what do I know? Zip.

All I know is this. We were storming the Eternal Gates of Chinatsu Yo, the rest of the Koro Ishi and me. We were on a roll, fighting back to back to back all eight of us, and then. Wham! I got disconnected. Snatched up and yanked out of *Gaijin Samurai* just when I was *this close* to the top.

Like, this ginormous Whatever yanked me out of the game and dumped me in this white brick oven with Father raving like an asshole and no way to tell my team why I left or where I went. My fucking phone is dead.

Dammit, we were on a roll. We were at the top of the Eleven Bloody Steps, me and the killer seven, my Koro Ishi. We trained together in the dojo and man, we're good. We slashed and burned our way to the Eternal Gates of the castle at Chinatsu Yo, we were *this close* when, shit! I, Hydra Destroyer, got sucked out of my avatar like a soul out of its skin without a second to explain. Now I'm marooned or whatever in white hell with a mess of townies I never liked, trapped in this freaking soup bowl with no way back.

Before it came down, me and best friends that I never met were fighting back to back— the Koro Ishi: Zorn and Takeda and Hajii, Xaos33, Exx, Marble, Eleanor and me, which, son of a bitch! We've played together for so long and fought so hard that we're, like, *fused,* me and them. It doesn't matter where we lived in the world or how long it's been since we did whatever we were supposed to be doing on what continent, we were connected in the game and we were *winning.* On the Eleventh Bloody Step, fixing to crash the Eternal Gates. We'd been playing all day and all night, it was intense. Once you're inside *Gaijin Samurai,* that's all there is. Players in the Koro Ishi know this: when you're winning, you'll blow off school or the day job, factory, office, wherever the other samurai from our dojo go in their pathetic shadow lives off-line.

This is all that matters. This.

I had the Dread Kobyashi backed up on the top step of the next-to-last level, one more blast and he fucking explodes. Hydra Destroyer, a.k.a. me, was fixing to flame Kobyashi and the Gaijinaut he rode in on into a thousand bloody bits, blazing fire from my seven mouths, I was magnificent. I had to kill him three times, and I was on number two. When I'm done and he vaporizes, I get to morph into Able Blacksmith with enough firepower to melt the lock on the Eternal Gates and we'll be in! Then and, like, only then, the Koro Ishi enters the three hundreth level in *Gaijin Samurai,* and believe me, we'll triumph in the Courtyard of Chinatsu Yo. Would have.

We were all, like, fuck sleep, this is too big. We're almost there.

Man, we were *this close.* When I got disconnected, Hydra Destroyer went out like a light and now. Oh. My. God.

6

Merrill

What is this, news or docudrama or something we don't know about? I'm not the only one strung taut, jittery and uncertain here. Exhausted by standing in one place, we fix on the screen, wondering, *Is it real?* Next to me, someone hisses, "Is this a movie?" while above us, the show goes on.

Here's Billy Maxwell in full uniform filling the screen, grinning like he expected to come back from Syria alive, although that photo is all Kara has left of him, and somewhere in the plaza, Kara Maxwell wails in pain— my best friend, and I can't get to her. Stacked like cordwood, stupefied by the heat, we hear experts expound on the great mystery. As though they've been studying our disappearance for weeks.

Wait. We just got here! Parched, dizzy and uncertain, I go a little crazy, trying to make it all make sense. Then Ned finds me in the forest of bodies. He socks my arm and I hug him in spite of himself. "Neddy, thank God!"

"Your phone!" He pounds until I let go. "I need your phone!"

I snap back with, "It's not like I sleep with my phone," ordinary Merrill for once, in an ordinary fight.

Tears pile up in his eyes. "I have to get back!"

I grab his wrist. "Look at me, Edward LaMar Poulnot. Were you up all night with that stupid game?"

Yesterday's manga T-shirt on him: Dark Warrior. Busted!

Tears pile up in his eyes. "I was *right there,* and now I'm not anywhere!"

Right. Chinyatsu Yo. I'm furious. "Is that all you care about? That stupid game? Neddy, look around!" *Oh, please don't cry.*

"I was so close!"

If you cry, I'll cry. "It's just a game, OK?"

"Shit no, it's my life!"

"Not now. It isn't even real." This is good for us both, getting mad at the same old thing. "This . . ." I grab his wrist and flick my nail at the long scab on his clenched fist.

"Don't!" He flinches. You'd think the wound was fresh.

Gently, I lift it. "This is real."

He snatches his hand away; the scab's so old that it hangs until he rips it off and bites down on it. Realization crosses his face in stages. The skin underneath is dead white. "Oh!"

Father pushed him against the stove and gouged that cut in him way back— when? Before. This is happening now. "See?"

"Oh, shit."

Oh shit. It's in the air, a hundred of us brought up short by the stone fact of it. *Oh, shit!* How could a thing like this happen to people like us? Nobody knows. *When* did it happen? Not sure. So this is when it hits me amidships. In this dead-white arena, time is elastic. Nothing is fixed.

On the screen above us, the show goes on, but we've had enough. When our questions and complaints get loud enough to mess up the audio, some intelligence cuts back to the channel islands montage, with wallpaper music swelling to calm us down. Then the pink nerf ball of a microphone pops up in front of the governor. He's speaking, but this is not his voice: "State troopers continue to scour Kraven island for survivors or . . ."

Drumbeat. As if to scare us into submission, the amplifiers blare. "Signs of violence."

To keep our attention, the banner running along underneath the feed expands to fill the screen— block letters, so there's no mistaking it: SIGNS OF VIOLENCE. It does the job.

Then everything rolls in on us all at once. The sun is a white hole in the white sky. The breeze has died and there are no shadows left. Stay here and we'll fry like marbles in a punch bowl, while above us, everything we've lost flashes by in a hasty reprise: our sweet waterfront, our abandoned houses, our empty rooms, our most intimate places laid open and magnified like specimens in a high school science class. All our abandoned toothbrushes, empty shoes and rumpled beds taunt us, everything we've lost and everything we care about . . .

That, I could have handled, but the agency behind our— what?— *removal*— wants more out of us. We are packed in tight, belly to butt, flank to flank, scared and flatulent and rank with morning breath, all Kraven island jammed in the plaza with no logic to it, local knowns and unknowns in uniform white scrubs, nobody any better or different from anybody else. We're all here except the one soul I thought I knew by heart. *I used to think I knew.* I whirl, yelling to fix what's broken, calling out again and again, and loud enough for my old life to hear and come back: "Up here Dave Ribault, I'm here!"

Then Ray Powell plants both hands on my shoulders to bring me down. "Merrill, shut up," he says, not unkindly. With the white hair and that big square jaw, he looks like a Roman centurion marching out. Immaculate Ray. When he speaks, you listen, but the day has changed him; I'm not sure how. He turns me to face the screen. As I turn with him, I see what Ray can't: Father, free for now, shoving people aside, hitting when he has to, anything to clear his way to open space.

I nudge Ray. "Father alert."

But Ray's fixed on the moving images above. "Shut up and watch. Help me figure this out."

If you think you want to know what happened to us, slouched in front of your TV or watching our story play out in your favorite bar or listening as your smartphone directs you through the streets of a strange city, I'll tell you who wants to know.

We do!

Sucked into the moving history, I lift my arms and jump high enough for Davy to see me in the crowd. *I thought I knew you.* I don't even know if they are watching on their screens back home, and it is bitter. *I don't know you at all. Dave Ribault, I . . .*

I'll never know what the *I* was because Ray snags my arm. "Don't!" I point to the cameras posted at all four corners of the plaza. "Please!"

"Right." We're on camera and too fried to wonder whether it's surveillcam or we're on TV. Ray boosts me higher, while Father bulldozes his way to the front. I should warn Ray, but I wave for the cameras with both hands, reaching. Praying, I think.

Ray puts me down. "Enough! Nothing we do will make any difference."

Looking into his bleak face, I see. I open my mouth and grief comes out in a groan. Around me, a hundred others let go too, and all our pain and confusion spills out in the plaza all at once. The sound is huge. Whatever we had been— blindsided by the experience, stunned, scared or mystified— turns into rage.

Electrified, Father climbs Delroy Root like preacher climbing into a pulpit and shakes his fist at the elements. His voice gets so big that it drowns us out. "Explain!"

He'll be blamed, but he's only the first. Like Father, Ray raises his fist. He turns to the camera, and shouts in a voice so commanding there's no mistaking who's the real leader here: "Explain."

In seconds it's a communal roar, a hundred Kraven islanders shaking their fists at The Power . . . if there are Powers, shouting: "Explain."

"Answers." Father goes on, at top volume. "We want answers!"

Well, he gets one. The TV feed stops.

And— like *that*— all telecommunications cease. In that second, we have made ourselves heard.

At that moment, we understood. Every television, cell phone, PDA and netbook in the compound is dead. We are mute, essentially deaf, blind and ignorant, cut off from life as we knew it, the struggling, imperfect, noisy real world. I flash on Neddy with his eyes rolled back in a blank face, replaying that stupid game inside his head, and for that half-second, I think: *Good.*

Good for Ned, sure, but without electronics, with no way to send for help or plead our case, we're stranded here, wherever *here* is. We can't search. Worse. We can't get a message out. Shaken, we turn on Father: *Look what you did,* we rage, terrified and livid. *In the name of God, shut up,* but as if nothing just happened he goes on shouting, "Explain!"

At which point all the scared, infuriated people Father mistook for followers converge on him, throwing whatever they happened to be holding when unseen forces yanked our lives out from under us— shoes, books, useless smartphones. Friends and neighbors close in on him, lawyers, probation officers and perps Father had put away while he was still a judge, women who hit on him after Mother left, *ordinary people we thought we knew* run at him in a rage, ready to bring him down.

Father is too enflamed to notice. Demagogue, on a tear. I know that fierce, contorted grin: *my people are angry*— his people!— the arrogant fuck. He spreads his palm on Delroy Root's face and hoists himself even higher, shouting, *"Tell them, people. Louder. Make them hear it. Crack the skies. Explain!"* Father rails on, shouting orders at the wind as the Dawson boys lunge and his voice cracks: "Order, order!"

He doesn't get it, but Delroy does. He sets Father down and backs away. The old man's mouth is still moving in the seconds before whatever civility we'd maintained so far shatters. Islanders fall on him, shouting, pounding, and I watch with OK, forgive me, a rush of vindictive joy. *Whatever they do, it serves you right.*

Then Ray smashes the empty bin against the flagpole, CRACK! The clang silences the mob and they fall back. Without speaking, he cuts through the crowd to help my father the yowling idiot who just made things worse. Ray picks him up by the armpits, sets him on his feet and steadies him with both hands. Knowing Father, I flinch, waiting for him to lash out. He shakes off his rescuer and stands straight, bunched to fight. Then he blinks. It's Ray. An extraordinary thing happens.

I see my father break in two.

He reels, shaken. His ugly mouth blooms in a beginning wail.

As it does, the giant speakers at four corners of the square come back to life, ending it.

ANNOUNCEMENT, ANNOUNCEMENT, ANNOUNCEMENT

We're so eager for news that everyone in the plaza falls still. We are standing at attention, but Ray has Delroy, Marlon Weisbuch and the Dawson brothers form a protective cadre around Father, just in case.

A hundred of us silenced. Docile for once, we fall back and wait to be told.

The next voice we hear is CG: an unseen animatronic group leader calls the shots. Chapter. Verse, a list of Things to Do by the numbers: One. Two. Three. We listen gratefully and line up to locate our quarters, designated on a map incised in the blank side of the main building.

First, we're to find our houses and move in. In that instant, the air in the plaza cools. As though something in the system changed it— sedative being pumped in? Too soon to tell. It could be the rush of relief that comes when you have places to go and something to do. Subdued, obedient for once, we study the map incised in the blank side of the main building. Anything to get away from the others, out of this square! Funny, how relieved we are to have certainties: marching orders in this mysterious, suffocating place. Scared and, OK, glad, to get out of that enclosure, we turn to go.

Ray stops us with a shout. "Wait!"

Even on Kraven, where we're relaxed and aggressively down-home, Ray gets what he wants. His people were in Kraven-town long before the Civil War; the Powell plantation took up half the island before his great-greats got enlightened and sold off everything but Azalea House and the grounds leading down to Powell's dock. He creates silence with a single word. "Friends!"

Heads turn. They always do. That's Ray.

"I won't keep you, but we need to talk." He puts his hand on Father's shoulder, making clear what we have to talk about. "Figure out how to make things right."

People catch the tune and echo like Baptists at a revival, agreeing, "We need to talk," "We need to talk," "We need to make things right!"

"Back here for a meeting, everybody. After we check out our new quarters and settle in. I'll get the word out when it's time."

He points to the building behind us, the big block letters mysteriously incised in its formerly blank face:

MEETING HALL

"Over there."

7

Davy
Thursday, late afternoon

Davy sprays smashed oyster shell, rushing back the way he came. *Slow, this is too*. Gets bogged down. *Too long*. Again. *Too damn long*. Foraging for dead branches and sprays from travelers' palms to get traction in the bad places, he consoles himself. Everybody else trying to cross Poynter's is either stuck in the five-mile stream of traffic backed up halfway to Charlton, or advancing on foot, swarming to join the mob at the causeway.

At least the shore road is deserted. *Better for me,* he thinks, not sure what he means.

Crazy, but at every bend in the road he stops and gets out of the car, fanning his phone like a mad witch doctor. Usually you can get at least one green bar out here, but things are seriously fucked up. He makes five stops before he can pick up a signal.

Naturally he phones home— rather, Merrill's cell. It rings and rings. He keeps trying, hitting redial the way you do when you're sure she's in the shower, has it on silent, dropped it in the car. Worst-case scenario, he'll leave voicemail. Anything to put them in touch. No Merrill. Worse, no voicemail prompt. No matter how long he lets it ring, no velvety Merrill message: "Whisper your darkest secrets here, and I'll get back to you." Davy persists the way you do when there's an incurable glitch.

Given what he's seen today and what little he knows, he keeps trying in spite of the reality that he's too messed up to admit.

It isn't only that Merrill doesn't pick up. Her cell is offline in some new, alarming way. It's ringing somewhere, somehow, but the threads that connect them are hopelessly snarled. He could hang on from now until the world ends and that's all it will do: ring. He fires off a text, in case. As if Merrill is anyplace he knows. As if she's in a position to text him back.

Where is she?

Her office phone is dead, the town hall switchboard is dead. So are the phones at home. Correction. At her house, is he still welcome there? Is every land line on Kraven island dead? He scrolls through every local number in his phone. He'll talk to anybody, friends, business contacts, cops, the twenty-four-hour clinic, whatever works. Nothing does. Yes he is not in his right mind. If he hangs in here long enough, he tells himself, somebody will pick up. *Unless they're all dead.*

His heart clenches. *Not them, Ribault. Not her, you idiot. The phones.* Again. Again!

It's like yelling into a cosmic void. He loves her, he can't reach her, he can't reach anybody on Kraven island and he needs to know what happened, where Merrill is, *how* she is; Davy is crazy with not knowing. He needs to go back inside himself and think, which he isn't doing very well right now.

Asshole. Get there.

Is he crazy, coming back this way? The crowd at the barricades was multiplying like cancer cells, ignorant gawkers mixed in with anxious homefolks and clueless supernumeraries with homemade armbands and TV crews, and the men in charge? Pit bulls and swamp things, most of them, like half the warm bodies in the county got rounded up this morning and supplied with an armband or a badge. One whiff of power turns them into armed forces bent on keeping the line they just drew. There are homeboys in uniform guarding the shore access ramps and homeboys at the causeway barricade, and the mouth-breathing knuckle-draggers among them are armed and resolute. People he knew and people he didn't know turned on him, breathing through their noses for once, with their jaws tight-shut and their eyeballs jittering like they'd just as soon blow your head off as not. He could turn back and charge the ramp again, he supposes, but for every Jack Stankey out there, there's an armed and dangerous Goethe brother or one of the Fripp cousins, twice removed, vigilante wannabes like Willie Deloach that used to slouch around school bashing kids' heads into locker doors.

Hell, he thinks, rolling across the rattling plank bridge at Pinckney Creek; a couple more miles and he'll be at Earl's. *Why did I not think of this, why the hell did I not think of this?* This is where he should have come in the first place.

He will damn well get home and find Merrill wherever she is, no problem, and he'll do it the best way he knows— by boat.

8

Merrill
Deep night

I still feel guilty.

I was so anxious to get shut of Father that I hurried toward the list of assigned quarters. I spotted my place at the far end of the map, at a comfortable distance from the one marked Poulnot, N., Poulnot, H.— just the way it is at home. Odd. On the map, this place looks to be laid out just like Kraventown. Odder yet. We were expected to stay where we were put.

This meant Father and my kid brother would be in the first house off the plaza, at the near end of the street leading out of the plaza. I didn't want to leave Neddy there— *where's Patrice?* But we had instructions. The air— whatever they pumped into the plaza— made it hard to think. I tugged at Ray. "Neddy. What am I going to do?"

"Right now, whatever they tell us."

"But. Father." I didn't have to explain.

He turned me back to the plaza. "Look at him."

Minutes ago, the crowd was ready to fall on him and beat him to death, but the air changed and for the moment, they forgot. They had orders. Places to go. Defeated, Father stood in the plaza with his head down, like a steer waiting for the knacker's hammer to put out its lights.

Our neighbors, *his people,* forgot, and it broke him in two.

Ray said, "He can't hurt anybody now," and he was right.

Father shuffled in place, blinking and confused, while angry islanders who had threatened to kill him took off, eager to find their places in this undefined new world. He stood with his head down, diminished.

Ray and I marched Father out of the plaza, with the Dawson brothers riding post. We delivered him to his new front door and saw him inside with orders to stay put. The old bastard went in with his head down, so stupefied that I had to wonder if he knew where he was. I couldn't wait to shut the door on him.

Then I turned and saw my brother's face. I tried, "You're supposed to." I couldn't finish.

"Not me. Not in there with him."

"It's on the list." I put my hands on his shoulders, but I couldn't find words. My mind ran to a dozen different places and came back with, *He's too far gone to hurt you.* It's true, but I felt bad, even thinking it. I couldn't find the right thing to say. It was awful. I blurted, "I just want you to be safe!"

"I can take care of myself!"

"You have to stay where they put you," Ray told him and then— does everybody know the old man is broken inside?— "It's OK, he can't hurt anybody now."

Shit, if Neddy cried, I'd cry . . . But he hung tough. "No way!"

Ray took him by the elbows, man to man. "It's your job. Until we find out what we've got here, there are certain things that we have to do."

The look Ned shot me broke my heart.

I think I said, "Hang in, kid." I hugged him goodbye for now and closed the door on Father and him, thinking, *At least he's safe.*

Ray went from door to door at twilight, collecting us. I went by the house assigned to Father and Ned. I heard the others fretting and grumbling, getting louder as they headed for the meeting hall. Feelings were high. Never mind what I felt in the moment when they turned on Father at the end of the long, hot half-day in the plaza, I ran ahead to warn him.

It was like warning a gargoyle. He sat like a stone in his new all-white dining room with his elbows planted on the all-white dining room table *in a house laid out exactly like our own.* He was drained of color. I could swear that his hair was turning white, unless it was a trick of the light.

"Father," I said, but he was too broken to look up. I did what I used to do when I had to get his attention. I tried to make him mad. I poked him, but he didn't budge. I baited him with, "Dad." I knuckled his bicep. "Hey, zombie man!"

He just stared into the glossy tabletop, too shattered to speak. Neddy jogged my elbow. "What's up?"

"I came to warn Father. He can't come to the meeting."

"Like he even knows there is one." Ned flew a hand past Father's face, doing that deranged bird tweet. "Like he's even here. So you're taking me, right?"

"Not really." What was I afraid of? You can't know the future, but you know enough to be afraid of it. There would be close to a hundred of us there, every one with a dozen different questions, conflicting ideas. Bad blood. If I said, You might get hurt, he'd say, I can take care of myself, so I said, "I think Ray said no kids."

"I'm not a kid!" *Oh Ned. Oh, Ned!*

"Besides," I said. "Father. It's important. Somebody has to take care of him."

"Father is over," he said. "Look at him!"

"Keep an eye on him, OK?" What did I think Father would do? You don't really want to know. "Just keep him here."

"Why?"

"I have a bad feeling about this meeting," I said. "I need you to stay back." I couldn't say, I don't want you to get hurt. I said, "And whatever happens, don't let him leave."

"Why?"

Everything bubbled to the surface. "If they see him, they'll tear him apart."

"Fine. Let them."

I said what I had to, to keep my brother safe. "Really. Please." Translated, *stay inside*. "For me."

Now we're here.

Inscribed above the building's double doors, the legend promises a possible end to our confusion. Assuming we can make them forget about Father, at least for now:

MEETING HALL

Outside, the bland, neutral face of the building is blank.

Inside, the pristine walls mimic our nineteenth-century clapboard grange hall on Kraven island. Some intelligence has ridged the brilliant white synthetic to make it look like whitewashed wood. Down front, a pulpit protrudes from the wall like a basin in some gigantic washroom, like this is church and if we wait long enough, somebody will climb up there and explain God. The stark white wooden benches are the only things made of anything natural in this pseudo American Gothic country church. As if every one of us will bow our heads and submit, or. I don't know. Cry to heaven?

No. As if we'll tell all.

Somebody assumed we were that docile, or that stupid.

Anyone with half a brain can see the cameras mounted in all four corners of the meeting room, with more cameras in the balcony above. As though we're dumb enough to squabble and scheme and play out all our confrontations, for the unknown audience.

That first night, we are that dumb.

People file in trashed and disconnected, a displaced, mystified community with everybody so scared, so wired and disrupted that they can't think anything through, not the cameras or what they're about or what happens when this many scared and angry humans come together in one place. The mood in MEETING HALL is toxic.

The worst thing about the night isn't them excoriating Father, muttering threats as they file in; he damn well deserves it. He did, after all, start the riot that brought on the electronic shutdown, but that isn't what sparks the fight. In highly charged situations, it's the small, stupid things that make people you thought you knew growl and struggle like a pack of werewolves in the middle of the change.

Inside, our neighbors mutter and jostle, strung tight and jonesing for an explanation, and in the void that yawns at the center of this sterile nightmare, theories swarm, buzzing like wasps, armed to sting:

"It's the government, they never explain," "No. Scientists, messing with us," "Chill, we're getting pranked," "Surprise, you're on TV." "Worse. It's Guantanamo, damn CIA got us for some crime we never did." ". . . gassed and airlifted to some heathen country God knows where . . ." ". . . high school kids from Walterboro, looking to punk the Charlton Tidal Wave." "It's the Chinese," "It's . . ."

Some woman— who?— shrills, "It's the hand of God!"

Ray's low, clear voice fills the hall. "We don't know what it is. That's why we're here. Now, hush," he says. He says into the silence, and for the moment, it works. "We're here to figure it out."

Then it doesn't. Jammed together like this, writhing with uncertainty, strung tight and miserable, our friends and neighbors self-destruct.

Big old Gert Taggart stands; she was an air traffic controller for years. "Don't worry. By now they're out looking for us, you know, just like that airplane, you know the one."

Rebel Dawson shouts, "How they're gonna do that?"

"Technology, asshole. Satellite cameras, sonar, drones, you know, all that stuff we saw on the TV, they can find anything on earth . . ."

Errol Root stands up, fixing her with those crazy eyes: "What makes you think this is earth?"

Gert overrides him, ". . . Like they're still looking for some in that building collapse, you know the one, not dead, they just wandered off . . . and there's some still out there from 9/11 that they never confirmed. We're just missing is all. They'll keep looking until they find us."

Missing.

I hear Kara Maxwell's heart break all over again. "They quit, but you don't. He's still out there somewhere, they just can't find him is all, so you don't give up." Bill Maxwell, Missing in Action, somewhere in Syria, unless . . .

"Shh, honey. It's not like that, but this is different. Hang in and *they will find us, they will!*"

"How they're gonna find us when we don't know where this is?" Marlon Weisbuch kept hold of his apron and tied it on over his scrubs, in a show of . . . go figure. He would have been firing up the grill when it happened, while Boogie opened the store, and where is Boogie anyway?

Errol Root yells, "We're in a fucking desert."

"Fucking A-rabs," Bud Dawson says, and it starts.

Gert shouts, "We don't know what's out there!"

Rebel shoves Gert aside and jumps up on a bench; his voice is huge. "We fight the bastards!"

She screams, "We don't know what's out there!"

"Look outside, assholes," Rebel says, knowing it's too dark to see anything. "It's *terrorists.*"

The men's voices rise, shouts overlapping. "It's the Russians." "The Chinese." " 'Od damn scientists."

"Towelheads, dammit," Rebel hollers, him with the battery of AK-47s in his armory back home, along with handguns and double-barreled shotguns that could take down a roaring bear. "WE HAVE TO ARM OURSELVES."

"Wipe 'em out."

Ray raises his arm and brings it down like a starter's flag. "Enough!"

"Kill 'em, whoever they are." "String 'em up." "Shoot 'em dead." "Kill 'em all." "Blow the place to hell." Rage spills over, reason obscured by the hundred voices that rise and overlap, melding into a mass *buddabuddabudda* that escalates, filling the room.

Until Gene Goethe, who hardly ever says anything, jumps up on one of the wooden benches, shouting loud enough to be heard over the fury, "Now, how are we going to do that?"

Rebel's voice overtakes his. "STORM THE ARMORY."

Then Jim Deloach drags Gene down off the bench and punches him in the gut and Rebel head-butts Jim, knocking him flat.

It's too late to reason. It's too late to do anything. We're stretched so thin that no one can say what we're thinking. Dislocated in time and space like this, nobody thinks. When systems break down and something has to give, what crumples is the personnel. Seeing Delroy Root's brother Errol going at Rebel Dawson over who will climb that pulpit and take over clinches it. Errol rips out Rebel's earring and the first blood flies.

Now our friends and neighbors morph into a mob. Fear and outrage collide and everybody in that hall sprouts fangs and claws. Men and women take sides, tugging back and forth over procedure until Ray's meeting explodes in a screaming free-for-all that ends in sobbing and smashed teeth, torn clothes and recriminations that rage on until everybody Ray and I had gathered to identify the problem and help us solve it is exhausted. Defeated by the explosion of frustration and raw fury, they can't organize themselves to strike another blow, unless . . .

Wait. The air changed. What did it? An infusion we don't know about or an unexpected chill? It's as if some new element entered the room and shut these people down.

Stunned by the sudden silence, people I know and people I hardly know tuck their butts under them like whipped hyenas and turn tail. Defeated, they go slinking off to their appointed homes, leaving Ray and me to— what?

At the end, alone in the wreckage, Ray and I study the mess. Our pristine meeting hall doesn't look so sterile anymore, what with all the snot and blood spots on the jigsaw of overturned white benches, and the plank that Errol broke when he threw down Rebel Dawson and stomped him. Our busted meeting is beyond fixing. The story is spelled out in bodily fluids smeared on the brilliant white walls.

In his time, Ray's seen everything, but tonight he's shaken. "We can't stay here." He means it on a dozen levels.

I'm probably more messed up than he is, so I hit on the one part of tonight that I can work with. "Not like this."

"And we can't leave it like this."

"Not if we want to get back to our lives. Oh, Ray. What are we going to do?"

"Whatever it is, we can't do it alone."

"Agreed."

"We need another meeting." He didn't have to say, "It's not about the cleanup."

"I know."

He says, "We can't leave it like that."

"Why not? You saw what they were like." In this new life, *people we thought we knew* turned into something else. Howling with rage, they took on like werewolves in the middle of the change, vicious and out of control.

In fact, by the time he and I sneak out hours later, with one exception every bench in the meeting hall is back in place, every white surface exactly as we found it when we filed in.

Shivering in the desert night, I ask. "What are we going to do?" My voice is a lot smaller than the space. I'm not scared, exactly, although there's that. I am struck by the enormity.

That we really are cut off from life as we knew it, alone in the dark in strange terrain, stranded in the great unknown.

That we have to find our way back to where we were— shit, to *who* we were— before it's too late, and they've forgotten us. Or everybody we've left behind has changed.

That we're being watched, probably recorded.

Jerking his head at the camera, Ray mutters, "We have to meet."

"We have . . ."

Ray grips my arm: *shhh*. He forms the words: "To figure it out."

It makes me shudder. *Not another meeting.* But this is Ray, so I mouth, "When?"

When he speaks his voice is so low that I can just hear it:

"I'll be in touch." Then he says aloud, as though none of this had happened, "Are you tired? I'm bushed."

This, I don't have to fake. "Me too."

He makes a broad grin for the unseen, all-seeing world, addressing the cameras like a third-rate actor. "Best money says, go home and get settled in."

"You got it." Big smile for the audience. "Night, Ray."

"Night."

We exit in tandem, two practiced hoofers leaving the stage. In the plaza we part company like two strangers and leave on two of the diagonal streets leading to the four corners of the camp, compound, whatever this is. It isn't hard to find my way back to the designated house. The ground plan is a lot like the one on Kraven island. As though the intelligence behind this— *removal*— mysteriously *learned* us, our patterns and our habits, mapping our small town down to the floor plans of our houses, before we came here.

We're not a random sample, no way. We were pre-selected for this . . . This disruption without a name.

9

Ned
Another night

Back home Father was The Power, but last week or ten days ago— whenever the real power came down and dumped us here, his power reared up and bit him in the ass, and dammit to fuck, I don't know when that was!

This place is so weird that I don't even know when *this* is. No clocks. I tried marking the days on my closet door but in the morning the marks are gone. **OK, so. If that's how it is** . . .

Patrice would love this place. It's, like, weirdly neat and anal-retentive clean. Necessaries like food and utensils come in by kitchen dumbwaiter as needed, and dirty dishes go out the same way. We get fresh scrubs every morning in the bathroom hatch. At least I'd have somebody here to talk to, you know?

The hell of it is, there are no books, no magazines, nothing in this terrible flat, white place to take your mind off it, no calendars, no clocks to watch. Our electronics are all broken and to make awful even worse, there's no TV!

And it's all Father's fault. This. Me, stuck in here with him. When Mr. Powell broke up the riot back on our first day, everybody from Kraven was like, *Damn you, Hampton Poulnot, with your big mouth and your Explain, like the only person in this universe is you.*

OK, when it started I thought somebody *would* come out and explain and that would be the end of it. Yeah, right.

After the great Whatever killed our electronics, it broke up Father's riot with a blast of white sound like one of those whistles only dogs can hear, except this one exploded deep inside my head. Then one of those CG voices boomed orders from all the speakers: What to do. Who did what. Which ones went to which houses. Where. And wherever they put you, you weren't allowed to move. **Your hand print is your door key. You'll find the site map on that wall.** They all ran like ants holing up in an ant farm, a hole for every ant, everybody into their hole.

I followed Mer over to scope the map and shit, it put me in this rotten house with Him. Mr. Powell and them dragged him here to this street. House just like all the other houses, deep-freeze white, tombstone front door. So the Dawsons grabbed Father's elbows and shoved him in quick, before the sun hit the top of the sky and roasted us to death and 'od damn if Merrill didn't pull me inside too, I don't care if she cried while she was explaining, if I never forgive her, it serves her right.

At least she came back that night, but only the once and I miss her, the bitch. She was all, "Are you OK?"

No fucking electronics, no explanation, fuck. 'Od damn I was pissed at her, sucked out of my avatar back home just when we were fixing to crack the Eternal Gates, I was more pissed at her than I was scared of anything. Usually I like Merrill, but I went all Hydra Destroyer on her, "You tell me if we're all right!"

"I can't." Then my big sister's face went eight ways to Sunday and I was like, *oh shit, Mer, don't cry,* but Merrill sucked it up. She stood on the no-rug in our nothing living room and stared into her dead phone and shook it and stared into it some more. Like it would ever ring and it would be her boyfriend on the line. Shit, he's my friend too, so where is he when I need him, right? She said, "I have to go to this meeting," but she rushed out like she thought she would find Davy in the night, well, good luck with that.

I wanted to go but she was all, *you have to stay back.*

Meanwhile, Our Father stared into the blank white tabletop, and it's not like he was looking for answers there. He didn't turn a hair. I grabbed the beard and shook hard, thinking to piss him off, and I went, "Well, Moses," like that would get him moving. "Are you supposed to preach at this meeting or what?" and if I thought they would snatch him bald-headed, well, fine.

I waited for his twitch that turns into a roar but nothing moved, not even the tight, white muscles around his mouth.

"If you don't go they'll sacrifice Merrill or start blaspheming and worshiping the Golden Calf or some damn thing."

That didn't get him. Nothing did. Either it's shock or that white noise thing fried his brain, he hadn't said shit since he ripped the sky with the big, "Explain!" and the screens went dark. It was kind of great, he was so convinced that for a second, everybody believed.

Then, **BLAM!** God, I was pissed at him. Everybody was. "So what are you, Father, afraid?"

He didn't even twitch.

"Well, I'm going." I opened the front door. By that time I was yelling. "And you can stay here and fuck yourself."

Noise came out of him then all right, it was bigger than the loudest "explain" but it wasn't exactly words, it was more like his guts were self-destructing and overflowing him like blood or tar, black sound. He surged up out of that chair like a shark jumping and flang himself on the door. He shoved me aside and shot the bolt. Then he fell across the threshold like a log and stayed there all night.

It's been days. I could go out to the rim and look for Merrill, except our windows are sealed tight and Father drops like a dead tree on that doorsill if he even *thinks* I'm fixing to leave, which he doesn't explain, but won't allow. It's not like Merrill comes over. Nobody does except Ray, he's all, *I promised your sister I'd check*. Then I go, *Well, why can't I go see her,* and he cuts me down with his eyes. **Because we don't know what's out there.** So, what? Does everybody have a petrified Father blocking the door?

Is it too hot out there, or too dangerous or what?

Well fuck me, locked in this white hell for ten days or whatever with nobody to talk to and nothing to but do replay Level 299 on *Gaijin Samurai* inside my head and wonder what's going on at Level 300, whether the Koro Ishi figured out how to crash the Eternal Gates without me or if they're milling around all helpless and discommoded, waiting for me at the top of the Eleven Bloody Steps.

This blows!

10

Davy

Thursday, late afternoon

When you've lived in these parts all your life except for the six years you spent at school in New Haven, you know everybody in Charlton and everybody on Kraven and practically everybody in between, and in the way of things in the low country, most of them are friends.

Then there are boon buddies, like Earl. Sucks that it took him half a day to figure out that he should have started here and the rest of the day making it back to Pinckney Creek and Earl's house, but he's here now.

Davy pulls his car into the woods, backs around, parking deep in the brush. If they find the car, they won't know which way he was heading or where he went. He ties his sneakers around his neck and rolls up his pants, thinking if the Poyntertown P.D. sends out Sidney and them in the Jeep to patrol the shore road, they won't know he's anywhere near the Pinckney place. Sweeping his footprints out of the dry sand behind him as he goes down to the water, he walks the rest of the way to Earl's house in the swash.

The look of the sand, the sky, the vegetation in the swash around the Pinckneys' dock take him back to Saturdays when he was a kid, pedaling out here on his bike to go crabbing with Earl. If they weren't best friends they were as good as, and that hasn't changed. Armed with a bucket of chicken necks, the string, the weights and the net, they used to wade into the shallows and scoop up enough blue crabs to guilt Earl's mother into making her amazing crabmeat thing. She made it with eggs and cream and a whole mess of cheese laced with enough port to get them pleasantly drunk. He remembers him and Earl taking the half-empty bottle out on the water afterward, two kids in a flat-bottomed boat, staring at the sky while they dreamed those dreams and talked that talk. In the years between they've been lucky enough to end up doing exactly what they wanted to do when they grew up.

Until today.

When things are going right, Davy's dreams turn into clean designs, houses, schools, comforting public spaces that satisfy his eye, and Earl, Earl splits his time between days out on the water and nights making music in his studio in the low-slung barn Gaillard Pinckney built back in the day— renovation designed by D.A. Ribault Inc. "I wonder what old Gilyard would think," Davy said when it was done.

Earl grinned. "He'd freak."

Now Earl hails him from the dock. "Dude!"

"Yo, Earl."

"You OK?" He waves in the general direction of Kraven island. "There's some big shit going down out there."

"I know." The weathered wood warms his feet. He smacks the heel of his hand into his old friend's shoulder, he's that glad to see him. "What the fuck, Earl? What the fuck?"

"'Od damn if I know. It flared up green."

"You saw it?"

"Mom did. She, like, wanders in the night?"

He knows that face. "Right."

"She saw it, but it's not like she can tell you what she saw.

Whatever it was, it set off instruments from here to east Jesus, starting with the surveill stuff over at the base. Time I got out in the boat everybody in God's creation was here: cops, troops, you name it."

"I saw."

"At least I pulled in this pike." Easy in a Market Street Crab T-shirt and cutoffs, Earl gestures at the filleted fish laid out on the dock at his feet. "Ma says it was on the TV before it crapped out, but it's not like she remembers."

It's not like she even knows if she did. "Is she OK?"

Earl grins. "About like you'd think. There are good days and bad days, but, dude. Did you not turn on your car radio?"

"Signal's all messed up. What's going on?"

"You live out there, asshole. You tell me."

"Wasn't home, can't get back."

"Oh, crap."

"It's not like I didn't try. Roadblocks, guards everywhere, all feisty and armed and dangerous. Your old bud Jack Stankey's holding 'em off at the pass."

"Shuh, that ain't the half of it," Earl says, slipping right back into it, talking the way they did, touch of this, touch of that, a little bit of Gullah in the overtones, just enough to signify that they know who they are and who their people are, two twelve-year-olds out in the boat, belching crabmeat and leftover port, same as it ever was. Except it's not. "Nobody gets on Kraven and nobody comes off of it. There's some kind of quarantine or embargo or some damn thing. It's all over the radio."

"Not mine."

"CB, dude, coastal band. I'm o' tell you, you can't get there from here."

Davy looks at the skies. Helicopters circle like angry bees feinting at the heart of Kraven island. "It don't stop them."

"Unelse they try to land."

"I need your boat, Earl, I'll keep care of it."

"Coast Guard's out there, so forget it, police boats circling low and vicious, like sharks."

"Not if I go around and come in from the ocean."

"Open water? They'll pick you right off."

"If I anchor on the far side of the sandbar, bodysurf in, they won't even know I'm there."

"Unelse you get caught in the rip."

"Riptide? Man, everybody knows how to get shut of that. Drop in at the right place and I can ride it until it spits me out pretty much where I need to be. You got an anchor in that thing?"

"Shut up, I'll carry you. Get in."

"Dude!" Davy strips down to his briefs and hesitates, passing his phone and his wallet from hand to hand.

"Put your particulars in here, you'll need 'em when you get stopped."

Davy's teeth clash and lock tight. "Nobody stops me."

Earl throws him the waterproof pouch. "Yeah, right."

"You drop me and take off instanter, right?"

"Fuck that shit." Earl hands down his tackle box and the bait bucket and jumps in. "Bluefish are running. Might as well drop a line while I cover you."

They're out on the water just like always, easy together, like nothing else is going on. For the moment it's so peaceful that when the sound of a remote explosion rocks Davy's head back on his neck, it picks him up and puts him down in a new place. He flashes on that classic scene in old movies— the party, the dance, the picnic where everyone's so happy that you know something awful is about to come down: *the last good time.*

Boom.

"Dynamite." He snaps back into himself. "They're sounding the lake."

Earl says, "To see what floats up . . ."

Davy doesn't want to finish it for him, but he does. "Because they're fixing to drag."

"For bodies."

"Fuck."

"Good news, asshole."

"How is that good?"

"It's almost dark. They're all over to the lake with their grappling hooks and shit, so nobody cares which way you come in or how you come in and they sure as hell won't mess with me, cool Gullah-man, wants him some pike. Keep low in the boat, you hear? Roll over and roll out when I tell you, and you'll end up at Powell's Inlet, halfway to Powell's dock."

They're so easy with each other that they go along in silence until it's time. Earl says, "I'll wait on you. Come back when you're done."

With one leg over the edge of the boat, Davy says, "Too dark. It's not like you'll know. Shit, I don't even know when I'll be done."

"Dude, how you're gonna get back?"

"Anybody's car." He eases himself over the side. "It's not like anybody needs it. They're all gone."

"Every shitass with a rifle's up there guarding the road."

"Anybody's boat," he says, and drops.

11

Ned
Anywhen

I had a whole world, and now it's just me and Father, Father
and me, and it's awful. He locked me in! It's been forever. Like
days. More like weeks, but in this white hell where I'm stuck
with him, who knows?

I'm trapped in here with nothing to do but wonder what's
going on back in the real world, i.e., the game.

Are they OK? Are they pissed at me?

What if they think I croaked at my machine, or that, I got,
like, *booted* for some heinous act I did that they don't know
about? I was fucking *disconnected*. Did they even notice when
I went POOF? Shit. What if they picked up another eighth, like,
that Secaucus Serpent guy from the Kendo Kadre that's always
trying to get in with us and played on through. They could be
storming Chinyatsu Yo right now, like there never was a Hydra
Destroyer.

Like there never was a me.

There kind of isn't, now. Just Ned fading into the woodwork,
one more white thing in a place with white everything: no rugs
on the bleached-sand floor, if you go barefoot you can pretend
it's the beach but shit, there's no curtains or pictures on the nub-
bly white walls and if they were, they would be white. It's like
color's not allowed— not even a fucking picture puzzle to take

your mind off it, whatever *it* is, like thinking will corrupt your soul. What are we supposed to, *meditate?* Plus, nothing to write on and nothing to write or draw with except your own blood and one other thing that it's too disgusting to try and if I tried it Patrice would have a cow, except she wasn't with us when we got took. Where is she anyway? Poor Patrice said Whatever to Father the other week and he smacked her so hard that he had to buy her a ticket up to her mama's house in Charleston to make up for it, so when it grabbed us, unlike me, Patrice got Left Behind.

Father's gone back inside himself and he won't come out. His fringe is turning into a great big Moses beard, like he's doing it to *match*. One more day like this we'll seize up like a Civil War monument. Gazillion years from now archaeologists will find us: Ned and Father alone in this white house in the bone-white silence, turned to stone.

He sits at that table all day and half the night in his white outfit with his white face buried in his white, white beard, all broody and stone silent, but I try. 'Od damn I try. I start a conversation between us every night, the problem being that the only one talking is me.

When the food comes, I start, "How was your day, Father?" but Father just chews.

Then I move around to the chair on his side and put on that deep, preachy voice, going, "Fine, son. How about yourself?"

My voice: "It's fucking bored out, Father." That's me doing what Father used to call "dropping the F bomb" so he'll get up and hit me like he does back home, but his fists don't clench. He doesn't even scowl.

I go back around to his side. "Language, Edward."

Me: "Don't call me Edward, I hate Edward."

I do a pretty good Father: "It's your grandfather's name and I will damn well use it."

"Don't be an asshole, Dad. You can fucking call me Ned."

Like Father ever answered to the name Dad. I thought two insults consecutive plus the "Dad" would bring him out. No, he gives me the bleakest look, but never mind.

I have a plan.

I've been working on this wall, behind the dumbwaiter? Stuff goes in and out through a hatch in the back, and I've been chipping away at the plaster every chance I get. So, what if there are zero jackets and shit in here, just the white scrubs, like we're patients in some ginormous hospital? I'm hoarding dirty scrubs. Tonight I put them all on, make some kind of hoodie out of the pillowcases. I'd rather freeze than fry, plus if they have guards or something, I'll be harder to see: white on white on white. Tonight, I break out.

I'm bailing just as soon as he sinks down in a heap at that table and starts to snore, but shit, I have to give him one last chance.

We eat. I talk for both of us. Then I do what I have to. I go: "Why did Mother leave us anyway?"

That stone face turns to marble, dead white. Then he breaks the Vow of Silence or whatever. It's like an iceberg cracking. "Go to bed."

So I do, but only until I hear him stomp away and crash on his bed so hard that it bashes the wall between our rooms. Then I open the kitchen dumbwaiter and break out the back and into the freezing desert night.

Back home on Kraven I used to run through the neighborhood reading other people's windows like comic books: the fight in one, the love scene, the bad little kids getting drunk, the beating in another, another and another, and everybody and everything in the houses I looked into was a different color, all blazing and busy like frames in a comic or the best animation you ever saw! The never-ending story occupied me on those empty nights before I found *Gaijin Samurai* and I logged on and had a life, but there's nothing here in this nothing place that we don't know what it is. Everything down in the great white toilet where we landed is still and quiet and white, white, white. White shutters on every window closed tight. The blank of the white buildings around the empty plaza are white, and the grainy white sidewalks lead out to white, white houses laid out like blocks on a Monopoly board with no colors and no printing and no squares so you can tell whether you're moving, just the bleached streets spreading out to the cement rim surrounding, as white and regular as a ring of false teeth without the gums or the grooves between. Even the barrier dune beyond is smooth and perfect, like a giant potter threw a porcelain bowl to put us in and the wheel stopped.

Nothing, not even the shadow of a footprint, touches the sand. It comes sifting down in the night wind and stops cold at the rim, so in spite of the breeze, everything inside it lies still.

That's weird, and this is weird.

There's almost no sound. Like it's one of those sensory deprivation tanks? Or it's some kind of prison, i.e., we are trapped, but there are no guards that I can see, no towers where armed guards could hide, nothing set up to keep anything out or any of us in, not like they need it, I'm the only person out tonight. Skittering like an ant trapped under a dome.

Alone. It's so *weird*.

So, what are they, locked inside against their will, like Father and me except he is, like, zombified, or are they all scared to go out?

It's cold as fuck out here, and darker than fuck, but! Free. I should be happy and excited, but I'm alone out in the open, and it's cold and creepy as hell. The silence is the worst. Like all the houses are soundproofed, unless nobody else is talking to each other either, same as Father and me.

There are no TVs in these houses, only one or two cracks of light showing around drawn shutters and nothing moving, as far as I can tell. Except for the breeze brushing the sand circle, there's nothing to hear.

Maybe it's like this in *Gaijin Samurai*, i.e., on Level 300 you lose your team, you lose your bearings, you end up with nobody to rely on and nothing to fight with except yourself and the great mess of *stuff* you know about, useless facts rattling around inside your head.

Is this place where we landed even *real life,* or is this the first level of a new, harder game I might not win? Yes, I am weirded out. And freezing. In another minute parts of me will start to break off like ice chunks in an avalanche. I can't stay out but I don't want to go in.

I just want this to be over, OK?

If I was ever Hydra Destroyer, that's done. I'm nobody but me, stupid Ned Poulnot, unarmed and unaided out here in the enormousness, shivering in my pathetic layers of scrubs, alone.

And then I'm not.

Alone. I mean.

There's a guy! He comes sliding down the inside of the barrier dune like a cross-country skier, easy on his feet and bone upright. He lands at the tippy end of the access road and gets up smiling and 'od damn, he walks toward me like the Thief that used to turn up in the old Xbox games and steal all your treasures while you were slaying the Avenger or recharging your Vector Belt, except he's half-whistling through his teeth the way you do— what is that tune? I hear him coming and this, at least, is kind of great. I saw him first. I know the tune!

I think it goes, "I'm just a lonesome traveler . . ." It stops.

Should I be scared? Hell if I know. He doesn't come on like one of us, from Kraven island, but I almost know who he is. He walks tall, not all cold and hunched over like me. As if he found a way to ditch the scrubs and get a real outfit, unless.

I don't know unless what, all I know is: tall guy walking fast, wrapped up in, is that a cape? Shuh, it's just a tarp that he ripped off something, but it's black. So are the jeans and thick hoodie— black boots, and that's cool, but it's also disturbing. How is he not shivering in the white scrubs like the rest of us?

"Fuck," he says, but not from close enough to scare me or near enough that I can make out his face. "What are you doing out here?"

"Who are you?"

He sort of laughs. "Me, scouting the perimeter like I was dead alone out here."

"See anything?"

"Nothing that would help."

"Who are you?"

"Friend of the family."

"Yeah, right." I like him, I hate him, I don't know how I feel except frustrated because he isn't saying, and even more pissed because I can't figure him out. "Really. Who *are* you?"

"Well, hell, who the fuck are you?"

"None of your business." By then I have him in my sights. If I was Hydra right now, I would . . . but I'm not, he's six foot something and I'm only almost fourteen. I show all my teeth like Father does when he's pissed off. "What are you doing here?"

He goes inside himself and comes back out with my answer, not his. "Oh. You're the Poulnot kid."

"Who says?"

"Little bird."

"Fuck that shit."

He just laughs. I'm meeting up with my first friend in this off-world new world and he sounds like all those smartass TV people up there making television in New York. "Hello, Ned Poulnot, pleased to meet you." He sticks out his hand.

Like I'm about to shake. "Hello, whatever the hell your name is."

"Steele. Rawson Steele."

Ohmygod. Oh. My. God. Everything I heard, all the ugly stuff people said about him back in Kraventown. Did he bring down the attack of the Big Whatever that yanked us out of our lives? Bad shit from deep inside backs up in my throat and like to strangles me. *You!* That guy, stalking our personal property like a prospector, did they erase us so he could get what he wants?

"What were you . . ." I want to say, *doing on Kraven island?* but I can't. I go, "What are you doing here?"

He sees the big question simmering, I'm like to explode and he puts up his hand real fast, to stop it, "It's not what you think!"

And then all the poison in me hits the top and blows the lid off. I lunge at him banging with both fists, and stuff comes spewing out of me but it's not exactly words, I am fucking sobbing, God, it is embarrassing. "You did it. You did this to us, you dumped us in this big white hell so you can go back to Kraven and take our houses and all our stuff . . ."

"Dude, I don't want your damn stuff."

"Well, you can have it, you can have our whole fucking island. Just get me out of here!"

"I only want what's mine."

"Mother*fucker*!" I'm shaking with it, where we are and how I was about to beat the game when this happened, and I bang my head into his chest like that will hurt him more and it finally comes out, "This is all your fault, it's your snot-blowing shit-licking assaholic fault."

I'm all acking and sobbing, I can't help it, can't stop it, until, *wham,* he rams a fist into my chest and knocks all the hate out of me.

Then he holds me off from him, waiting for me to settle, and when I quit struggling he lifts me up off the ground by about a foot and holds me in place until I finally get my breath back and sob it all out, and quit even trying to kick.

He holds me off a minute longer and when it's clear I've vomited out all the *angry* backed up inside of me, he sets me down and we stand there looking at each other until I start shivering because losing it warms you up, but not in a good way, and not for long. "Oh, kid." He rips off his tarp and wraps it around me and I let him. "Be sure and hide this when you get home."

"That isn't home."

"I know."

Then he looks at me straight on and says to me, like we are two grownups, "I don't know how we got here or what did it." His voice is all cold and so still that it scares me silent. "I don't even know what this place is."

12

Merrill
Anywhen

Time blurs in this place— no clocks or calendars, no phones and no other ways to check the time, just light and dark and food in the dumbwaiter three times before the sun goes down, which we have to assume marks real days and real nights. As though this is no state in no known nation, just a state of mind.

So I can't say exactly when Ray Powell and I finally reconnected, only that the other night I heard somebody whistling in our dead little world of epic silence and when I came outside, it was Ray.

My shadow house here sits exactly where my real house did on Kraven island. It's laid out in the same footprint, but unlike my place with its long front porch and jigsaw trim, this one turns a blank white face to the barren street. As I opened the door, the whistling stopped. I slipped outside the circle of light on my front walk and there was Ray.

I whispered, "You're outside!"

"I am."

"Then it's all right."

"So far." He drew me out into the middle of the street, too far from the lampposts for their spyware to pick up anything we muttered in the dark. In our situation, you pre-suppose watchers stationed somewhere, studying a hundred monitors. Ray and

I leaned close, for reasons. Let them think we're lovers sneaking out, not the only two prisoners sharp enough to collude.

Yes I said prisoners. What do you think we are?

Ray's even older than Father but he doesn't look it. Unlike Father he comes in smiling and he's aggressively fit. He hates argy bargy, so he ducks town meetings, but things work better because of Ray. Like his father and grandfather, he works behind the scenes. For generations, the Powells have shaped Kraventown, moving generations of hardheads like Father so smoothly that they don't even know.

If the intelligence monitoring our displaced lives found out who Ray really is and that we're in this together they'd lock him up, shut us down or worse, ergo the faked assignation. Our town's been hijacked. We have to figure out what's going on and what comes next. That night I put my arms around Ray's neck because I trusted him and romance seemed like the best disguise. In the real world, Ray's safe as houses. No. Ray Powell is safe as a temple of stone. I stood quietly in his arms, waiting for him to start. He bent as though we were kissing, muttering into my ear, "We need a plan."

"I know." Even standing close like that, we were shivering. The night chill penetrated to the bone.

"As in, find a place and call a meeting."

"A meeting," I said bitterly. "After what came down last time?" Resentment hung in the air between us like frosted breath.

Ray rubbed my arms, but it didn't help. It was so cold that his voice rattled. "We can't do this alone."

"We can't do it with them, not the way they are." I could still taste the blood in my mouth.

"Were."

"It was awful."

Blood in my mouth and blood in the meeting hall; it was disgusting. Filthy smears on the walls after Ray broke up the fight and the others left. That night we cleaned up in silence and walked away from certain indelible stains. We were done for the night. Done with them. Done in.

"They're our people, Mer."

"They're awful."

"Were. This place," Ray said, without explaining. "They've changed."

The rest rolled in and hit so hard that I fell back a step, couldn't breathe. Then it came in a rush. "We've changed."

Ray said, "You OK?"

"Not really." I swallowed pain. Ray had promised. "Is Ned?"

He nodded. "So far. Merrill, we need the others." He put his big hands on my shoulders and leaned hard, grounding me. "Don't ask me how I know this, I just know it. Either we all go or nobody goes."

The next day we went from house to house in the blistering sunlight, trying to rally them. We kept knocking on doors until it got too hot to be outside. We thought our neighbors would be jonesing for another meeting with questions answered, questions raised, but what can I say?

They blew us off.

They blew us off, one after another.

The few who opened their doors were passive and glassy-eyed. Stunned, as if they'd just been hit by a truck. They don't go out and they won't let us in, not kind, responsible Ray Powell, that the community admires and respects and *owes* in a lot of ways, and, even though we all have history— we grew up together!— not me.

It didn't matter who I tried or what I said, I got back flat refusals shouted from behind closed doors, with one or two whispered apologies leaking out between the cracks. Every day was harder, probably because every day the sun burned hotter than it had the day before. The few who opened their doors to me were friends like Kara Maxwell and Betsy Till, people I thought I knew but don't, not really, not the way they are.

Seeing Kara was the hardest. "Oh," she said and her voice sank, "I thought you were here about Bill."

"Bill's missing."

"So am I." Her face crumpled and she wailed, "How is he going to find me here?"

"Oh, sweetie!" I put out my arms but I couldn't reach her.

"Don't," she said. I knew that look: *Some day they'll come marching down our street.* It meant, *don't say anything more.* My best friend Kara shoved a bottle of water at me. Her eyes were spinning like marbles and she fell against the door, shutting me out.

A guard in high school basketball, Betsy Till stood in her doorway waving her arms, waiting for me to feint, and Selina Crane? She snarled like a tigress shielding her cubs. Old Mrs. Tanner and the Weisbuchs were nicer because they remember me when, but they're too shaky to come out in this heat and terrified of letting anything in. I was touched that Tappy Deloach even got out of his chair and made it to the door. I guess they felt sorry for me, soldiering on, all dehydrated and anxious and trying to smile, parched and panting in the heat.

Ray did no better.

I have this fear that mysteriously whisked off-island and set down in a rigidly structured landscape so far from the Inland Waterway that we can't see the ocean or hear it or even smell the salt, the displaced population of Kraven actually likes being contained.

Ray thinks they're all in shock. He says removal and alienation took apart people we used to know and put them back together differently, although that doesn't explain him or me. Even the town loudmouths like Errol Root and Wade Tanner won't come out. This place made them get a lot smaller, apologizing from behind half-closed doors. Rebel shot his big arms across the opening like bolts. Trauma keeps them inside. These houses are designed for comfort. Contained, our people are safe from unknown hazards— their neighbors and their enemies, scary outside entities that they don't know about.

I think they're victims of the design. Whoever did this to us built the compound with security and comfort in mind. Then they set it like a trap and sucked us into it. Uproot a group and while you've got them flailing and terrified, enclose them. Keep them clean and fed and they've settled in: snug houses secured against the elements, everything we need supplied so we'll forget our *wants*. Hermetically sealed calm. New food appears in our kitchen compartments at mealtimes, fresh linens show up in the cubby next to the basin once a week— more often if needed. There are fresh scrubs in our closets every morning, neatly folded on shelves above the chutes where we dumped our ruined clothes from home at the end of that terrible first day.

Maybe there really is some strong drug in the food or air or in the water, but if that's it, how come Ray's still Ray and I'm still anxious, fucked-up me?

When all about us have lost it, why are Ray and I still functional? Why, in a community of one hundred, are we the only ones with the guts— no, the psychic energy— to come outside? Granted, the sun burns hotter every day and nights are cold and dark and, OK, scary. Nobody with any sense wants to come out in this, but Ray and I are driven, and not just by our wants, I don't think.

We're driven by need.

I need to get back to Davy or to get Davy back, I'm not sure which, all I know is that to settle this, to talk it through, we need to stand so close that we can see inside each other's heads.

Ray won't tell me what, exactly, pushed him to the edge where he balances so neatly, taut as a ropewalker. "Urgent business at home," he told me the one time I asked. He wouldn't specify, only, "Tell you about it after. Not here." He was tendering the unspoken agreement.

I signed and sealed it. "Not here."

OK then. We'll keep at it until we beat the game, crack the code, uncover the plot or trap one of our keepers and shake the truth out of him. We'll arm ourselves, fight to the death if we have to— whatever it takes to crack out of this weird existential jail.

We meet at the tag end of most days, after the desert plunges into darkness but before the deep night chill drives us back inside. We scope out new areas. We speculate and collude, and for whatever reasons, the organizers of this— what, experiment in living? Psychological study? Sadistic peepshow?— let it play. The organizers or monitors or keepers, whatever they are, don't interfere. Unless they don't notice. Or they notice and don't care. Unless this is part of their plan. Speculation feeds on itself and we worry the question to death: if there's a plan, what, exactly, is the plan?

Shrouded in the blankets from our narrow beds, Ray and I look like a couple of kids out playing ghost, so it's not like we're hard to spot. In the territory beyond the plaza, there are cameras in every block. Clearly they know we're out here, but in the last three weeks nobody, armed or unarmed, has come out to stop us and no automated *thing* has rolled out to intercept and herd us back inside.

After that first venture we cut holes in our blankets and made ponchos so we could come out in the dark without turning to ice and shattering on the spot. Fresh blankets appeared in our cubbies the day after we vandalized ours, but the makeshift ponchos stayed where we put them, along with the layers we've added since. Neatly folded replacements show up on our beds with creepy regularity. Are they trying to warn us or encourage us or reprogram us, organize us, or what?

The cameras can follow us, but only up to a point. There's an island of shadow on every street, the place where circles of light don't quite meet, and Ray Powell and I take a different route to a new island of darkness every night. We meet regularly for tense, whispered exchanges and so far, nobody's intervened, not our neighbors cowering in their houses and none of our handlers— if there are handlers— and nobody in the audience— if there is an audience.

We talk in circles. Speculation and escape plans chase each other's tails so fast that like time, everything blurs. Sometimes I think we're contestants picked from some vast studio audience and called onstage, front and center, to star in some monstrous reality show. "Like, they'll give us all cars and lifetime cash prizes if we win." I hear my voice cracking, "You know, push the right button, take down the enemy, break out."

Ray says, "Unless they're running us like rats in a maze."

"Or we're stuck in a gigantic RPG."

"A what?"

"Role-playing game." Oh, Ray, how old *are* you? "You know, like giant kids with joysticks are operating us?"

"You mean messing with our heads."

"Oh shit, Ray, what if they end this show or whatever by putting you and me in the plaza and we have to fight to the death?"

Good old Ray grounds me. "We won't."

"But what if . . ."

"No. It's an experiment. Either they study us and dissect us or it's a psych thing where they evaluate us and write a report, and when they're done, we go home . . ."

"Changed." I don't know why this comes out as a groan.

"We're already changed." This is how he brings me down. "We can sit here mizzling or we can plan."

So these nighttime encounters boil down to figuring out what comes next: mounting an escape or, worst-case scenario, getting a message out so no matter how this ends or what becomes of us, somebody will know.

Until then, there's this. We go out every night. Whatever our days are like in those sterile houses, Ray and I are free in the night-time world, at least for now, plying back and forth in the dark, exploring our changed lives, and like everything else, this operation runs on hope. Maybe tonight we'll find one of our handlers or suppliers— whoever keeps this operation running— surprise the bastard at work. In the kitchens, which we have yet to find, or in an office chair in the blockhouse, fixed on banks of monitors. We'll stalk him and nail him down and hold him until we get answers.

We search, but the barren desert streets give me the sad, sick feeling that everything is automated here in the bland magic kingdom where days and nights run like clockwork, with everything supplied and everybody but us either scared to go out or drugged or what passes for happy, resolutely staying inside.

Once we thought we saw a figure darker than the shadows whip around a corner in front of us. *Neddy!* I had to swallow my heart. I wanted it to be him, I wanted it not to be him because he's just a kid, not tough enough to be all by himself out here in the cold. I've kept him at arm's length because I have to keep him safe. He's big for his age but he's still my baby brother, and too damn young to be trapped in this awful, preternaturally clean place.

Ray and I slipped around the corner after who or whatever we thought we saw, thinking to follow without him knowing we were following. We skulked along behind the fast-moving shadow, zigzagging all the way from the plaza to the rim, but when we came out of the shadows at the boundary where pavement gives way to the surrounding dune it was dead empty, same as it ever was.

Again last night I thought I saw him; maybe it was guilt. I hissed, *"Neddy!"* and gulped it down so he wouldn't hear. I can't have him running around out here in the night; we don't know what's out here, or what it will do to us. I miss him. I'd give anything to see that grin, but after everything, he won't want to see me. Sorry, Ned, I owe you an explanation, but first we have to get you home. Then I'll sit my brother down and explain a lot of things, starting with why I won't go back into that bleached cube where he and Father stay.

I can't talk to my brother there, it might jump-start Father and bring him back to life. As long as the old man is sedated or whatever it is that's turned him to stone, Neddy will be safe.

Tonight Ray and I haunt the shadows on yet another street leading away from the plaza, floating uneducated guesses and coming up empty one more time.

Then Ray grabs my wrist. He doesn't have to speak: *Listen!*

We stop breathing. Ray cranes, trying to see beyond the next corner. I crack my jaws wide, desperate to hear.

Nobody says, *what was that?*

No one has to. The sound is unmistakable; it's the plastic clunk of a cell phone, hitting cement and skittering to a stop. Startled, somebody rasps in a voice I almost recognize, "Shit!"

13

Davy
Thursday night

Ray Powell's house is as fine as any plantation house on St. Helena's or Pawleys' Island. From the water, the Azalea Plantation looks so perfect that if you didn't know, you'd think you'd landed on one of those high-end resort islands where everything runs smoothly and nothing goes wrong.

It took generations of Powells to create this monument to the way things used to be. Ray's great-great great-grandfathers built the house in the 1800s and prospered, leaving enough money for Ray to go up north to Charlottesville for college and law school at UVA like his forefathers, mixing with all the other sons of the South's first families. Like the other great-greats who settled here, the Powells are obligated.

It's a matter of *noblesse oblige,* the idea being that God put the Powells on Kraven island to be leaders— and to keep the main house at Azalea more or less as it was in 1898. That was the year Augustus Powell gave up planting for politics. On his way to the election that put him in the State House, he brought a Charleston tailor to Kraven to build him a handsome three-piece suit, trimmed his beard into a neat goatee and sold off all but the land between the inlet and the gardens around Azalea House.

By the time Davy skins out of the water and up on Powell's

dock, he regrets leaving everything but his briefs on Earl's dock. Red welts are rising on his naked flank: *cannonball jellyfish,* he thinks. *It's not so bad.* Without Earl's waterproof belt Velcroed to his waist, it would have been worse, so he may be wet and near naked, but he's OK. As for Kraven island, it looks the same. So does Azalea House. Standing here in front of Ray Powell's house with its generous porches and wide steps coming down to greet you, you'd never know there was anything wrong on Kraven island. The air's just as sweet as it was yesterday— God, was it only yesterday?— but the island has gone silent. The gulls are gone. Even the insects and lizards inhabiting the marsh are still. *One explosion too many,* Davy thinks, because he's strongly aware that on the other side of Kraven island, authorities from every island and hamlet are dragging the lake. As if his friends and neighbors— his lover!— turned into lemmings, rushing down to the lakefront in a body because they got up at dawn today for no known reason, thinking to hurl themselves in. *Lemmings. As if.*

People like us don't wander out of their houses, ditch their cars, partners, house pets, rowboats or whatever at the exact same hour, struck by the exact same death wish, simultaneously going out of their universal group mind and out of our lives. *Impossible,* Davy thinks, but who knew that everybody he cares about would up and vanish, every fucking one of them gone from here, WHAM! Gone soon after he sneaked out of Merrill's bed and left. *Oh shit, I should have left a note.* As soon as he's done at Ray's he'll go home and apologize.

She'll be all ruckled up and pissed off at me, like, "Where have you been all day? What took you so long?"

If he's so sure Merrill's back home, more or less where he left her, why is he here on Ray Powell's front walk, waiting to be told?

Davy heads up the wide steps, thinking, *Ray will know what happened. He always does.* They're closer than he was to his father, as in, a friend Pop's age; they can hang out without family baggage getting in the way. Ray'll find dry clothes for his creeped-out friend, standing out here barefoot and shivering in his briefs. His belly clenches. There will be food. So what if everybody else up and took off? He can always count on Ray.

The front door stands open to let in the breeze. Ray would never take off without closing it, so he's definitely home. The screen is latched, no problem, Ray's always glad to see him, no matter how late it is, all he has to do is ring and Ray will come down from his third-floor office and open up. They can sit down over leftovers: whatever Ella made for his supper and Ray will explain everything. Davy comes to himself with a start. *How long have I been standing here?*

He yells. "Ray!" He tries the bell.

Here's the problem: from here, Ray's house doesn't smell the same, which is even worse than the silence. Ella DeVine's usually in there after supper, making biscuits before she leaves; she lives on Poynter and comes back at noon to fix his lunch. *Shit, when did I eat?* His naked belly contracts. Oh, there'll be biscuits, yes, but what's cooking, really? Nothing tonight. He can hear the bell ringing deep inside. He takes his finger off the button and pounds on the doorframe, yelling, "Ray, it's me." After too long, he follows with, "Are you deaf?" In the end, he has to punch a hole in the screen and undo the latch. Maybe Ray really did go deaf while he wasn't looking, he thinks hopefully. It's been a while. *As soon as I clear the door he'll jump up from the supper table and apologize,* he tells himself, padding down the long, empty hall to the dining room, *maybe he really is going deaf.* Ray's the one person on Kraven that he can count on, especially now.

Better not walk in on Ray gasping, "Thank God you're here."
Ray would be mortified, so he calls, extra loud, in case:

"Ray? Yo, Ray, it's me! Just so you know, I'm near naked."
Shivering in the twilight breeze, he notices the dreadful symmetry of the carpets on the polished floors in the long front hall, the sinister butterfly pattern on Ray's wallpaper in the waning light.

With nobody answering and nobody around to tell that he's here, he stops outside the dining room door to collect himself. Try to sound casual, going in. "Yo, Ray." If he's here! "I'm not rightly dressed for dinner, but I'm fucking starved."

There's nothing of Ray here except his half-eaten breakfast. While he was standing out there temporizing, the sun sank, and in this light, it's hard to make out what Ray left on the plate. Reluctant to eat anything he can't see, Davy picks up the Brookstone fire-starter Ella uses and lights a candle.

Ray's stuff has been sitting here for more than a while: abandoned coffee, half-drunk, and Ray gets up at five. Soft-boiled egg cracked open in the china egg cup, with the punctured yolk congealing on its spoon. There are eggy smears on the willowware plate, along with a biscuit minus a half-moon chunk where Ray took a bite. Davy stuffs it in his mouth, drinks the cold coffee and ravages Ray's silver bread basket for more, feeling guilty and shitty for being here when everybody else is missing or abducted or they all ran away from whatever it was— unless they just took off for unknown reasons, but, hey.

He doesn't know what's gone down or comes next. He just knows he has to be strong.

He hisses through his teeth as he heads upstairs, a hopeful threnody that keeps him going, alone in a deserted house. *Ray's here, he has to be. Could be he got caught short and fell in the bathroom, good thing I'm here to help,* and, on the landing,

Right. Ray isn't hurt. He's fine. He's up there in the attic right now, he got hung up in the Internet, looking for answers. He's that kind of guy. *Ray won't quit until he figures it out.*

Davy knows in his heart that Ray is nowhere in the house, but he opens the door to the attic anyway. "Take off that damn headset and get down here, Ray Powell. Something awful just came down."

What comes down is silence except for claws skittering, probably squirrels. That and maybe ghosts of the dozens of escaped slaves Ray's ancestors hid in the warren of attic rooms. Naturally the Powells had slaves, they were Carolina landowners, but that all changed well before the Civil War. Because the Powells are who they are, Ray's great-great-greats established an underground railroad stop up there, where runaways stayed until it was safe to move them out by boat.

If it was that hard sneaking those few souls off Kraven island back in the day, Davy thinks, *how did a hundred-some people exit Kraven this morning and nobody knew it was happening until it was too late?*

Yes, he is hung up on it. How. The why.

Don't. Shaking off doubts like a dog tormented by horseflies, he shuts the door and heads down the hall to Ray's room. Sticks his head in, saying politely, "Don't freak, I'm near naked. Sorry about that," he says to the silent bedroom because he's had too much of silence. Louder. "I need clothes before the skeeters carry me off." Louder still. "It's no big deal. Just some old shit you don't need and never wear?" and when nothing happens, pads on in, flexing his toes in the lush, blue-green wall-to-wall.

There is no old shit in Ray's thickly carpeted dressing room but there is a flashlight, so he can lose the candlestick and use this until the bulb dies, which it's about to do. The shelves of freshly laundered shirts and neatly folded sweaters, shoe racks, tie racks, rows of jackets, suits, freshly ironed jeans and khakis reproach him. *Look on my works, ye mighty, and despair.* Who scrubs his deck shoes, pairs them and lines everything up neatly on the built-in shoe racks? He sticks his head into Ray's bathroom. It would almost be a relief to find him lying there, but there's nothing and nobody to break the white surfaces: tile, white porcelain toilet and basin with a marble lip, period white tub with all four feet planted on its marble pedestal, perfect. Empty. *Stop looking. Stop hoping. Get out of here.* Grabbing a T-shirt and some pristine Dockers, he reaches for Ray's oldest topsiders. The underwear? Too intimate, it would be like putting on another person's private life. Embarrassed, he brushes his way out of the master suite and into the hall, erasing the prints his bare feet made on the thick rug. He drops Ray's flashlight on the floor in the hall and at the clatter, hisses, "Shhhhh," *Shit, did I just apologize to that thing?* Oh, yes he is getting weird, and weirder still is the raw scrabble of claws on bare wood. Roused by the noise, somebody or some big *thing* is coming down the attic stairs. *Too big for squirrels,* he thinks, *raccoons or possums breeding in the sofas. If I can't find Merrill and get her and Ray home, there's gonna be God knows what-all nesting up there.*

If they don't come back I'll just.

He doesn't know, but the rest of the sentence comes to him unbidden. *Die.*

Scrabble, THUMP. Whatever it is, the thing in the attic just threw itself at the door to the hall where Davy stands. OK, something is better than nobody. He opens the door and the critter launches itself.

"Thank God it's you," he tells Ray's red setter, what's that dog's name, Towser, Bowser? He doesn't know. "Dude!" They hug for a nice minute with the dog's forepaws planted on his shoulders while it licks and licks until they teeter and Davy lets it down on all fours. He squats on the floor and leans in, grateful for the setter's warm head and its big, messy tongue lapping, lapping; the dog is just as happy to see him. Ray's flashlight gives out, but it's OK, he has the— dammit, what is this dog's name?

He stands. "OK, Dude, let's go."

It's that little bit lighter outside than in. It's eerie, slinking through his adopted home town like a space alien or some kind of halfassed spy from a country we didn't know we were at war with.

Padding along like a trouper, the Dude follows: proof of the existence of Dave Ribault.

Bay Street is the worst. The history of his life in this town in three blocks. For God's sake, he expects to marry Merrill in Trinity Chapel over there, he just hasn't figured out how or when or, shit, whether— which, OK, leaves him feeling guilty because their unfinished business sits heavy on his heart. The Marlin Boat Club, where they would have the wedding dinner because Merrill loves it there. They'd have a cake from Tansey's and Kara and Ray standing up for them. Champagne from the Bottle Shop and music by the Empty Pockets, yes. He dodges into an alley because he can't think about that anymore.

All the island's lights have gone out. Even the street lamps are dark, but there is a police presence: emergency lights at the roadblock, one state trooper patrolling, one cop pacing back and forth across Bay Street. Police cars and the TV truck stand empty.

Whatever happened here yesterday was huge and, Davy thinks, the removal of a population this size can be— must be traced back to a solid, physical cause. Somebody or something found a way to scoop up every living human on Kraven island and— what?

Transport them.

Whatever the machinery, it yanked his life out from under him like a rug. They're all out there somewhere, Davy's sure: Merrill and Ned and their monolithic father— everyone who belongs here, same as they ever were.

Wherever they are.

While he personally is on autopilot, slouching along side streets and back alleys with no idea what he's looking for or how to find out what he needs to know. He comes back into himself on Poulnot Street with a start. He's almost home. If he lets himself into Merrill's house and does all the usual things, he thinks— how long has it been since he ate?— if he can just sit down in her kitchen long enough to refuel; if he can crash on their bed and snap into fetal position and sleep, in a few hours the sun will come up like it always does, Merrill will be there and this will end.

If only.

This is no bad dream. The disappearance was too complete, with many moving parts that clicked into place on cue. It had to be produced, he thinks. Like a show. If he's right, in a couple of hours he'll wake up to banked studio lights, a camera crew because, hey dude, you're on TV. Smile for the audience and you and your girlfriend here . . .

Shadows breed paranoia. *That handsome, shady bastard I caught hitting on Merrill, I saw them.* He saw, but he doesn't know what he saw. *What if she's in on it?*

You bet he's getting weird. Right, he tells himself without conviction, yesterday never happened, this whole exercise is just that: highly competent reality TV, with a leering, smarmy game-show host just waiting to spring the truth on him while a cast of Kraven islanders cheers as he and Merrill— what?

Rush into each other's arms with joyful cries or recriminations. He is too wild and confused and, OK, guilty, to guess which.

Passing the neighbors' empty houses is terrible. For him right now, they reek of missed chances, disorder and recent sorrow. Loneliness, he thinks. Sad. Places look as if every last one of them was caught unawares, removed helter-skelter, half-dressed and unprepared.

For the confused fool left alone in this tight little world, the universal absence is terrible: close and personal, he thinks in a wash of guilt. Like it's something he did. He and the dog go along to the house where he and Merrill live. Lived.

He shakes himself awake. *Fuck I'm tired. How long have I been standing here?*

Standing on that porch in, OK, a weakened condition, Davy groans as the trouble he's tried so hard to outrun comes back around and smacks him in the face: the fight. Before any of this came down, he and Merrill had a fight. They tangled in her kitchen after midnight, bitter words he's too fried to recall. When she came back to bed much later, shivering and distraught, Davy rolled away from her, faking a snore because he was too miserable and conflicted to think it through and say the right thing. Too stupid to figure out what the right thing is. Instead he crept out while she was sleeping, to keep this assaholic appointment with Rawson Steele in downtown Charlton.

He let her sleep and now she's gone. They're all gone.

Look, when he got home after that long, totally crap Wednesday, he spotted his woman and Rawson Steele with their heads together under the yellow porch light like lovers colluding. They jumped apart as he burned gravel turning into the drive. Steele was gone before he could reach the porch— what was he, guilty?

Guilty of what? Davy's ashamed of the things he said to Merrill after he rushed her inside and slammed the door.

"I love you," she said, running her hands along his shoulders. She'd explained, but he was too mad to remember what she told him, except, "Oh, lover, he can't help it."

Then she whispered as though the bastard was still within earshot, "It's weird, but he's just another poor, sad Northerner, down here looking for his roots."

He forgets what he said back, but he'll never forget Merrill's face when she cried:

"Really, it's not what you think!"

He should have apologized. No. He should have asked her what about it was weird, but he was too pissed off to ask and Merrill was too hurt and angry to explain. They ate takeout so they could talk about what to order. They found busy-work to keep from having to talk. For the same reason, they watched bad TV. They went to bed and slept not much and after midnight they collided in the kitchen and had the fight.

"Davy," she said when they finished, and she was shouting, "if you're that fucking paranoid, you can either marry me or move out," and that's the last thing she said to him.

He sucks in his breath. Lets it out. "OK, Dude."

The dog follows him in.

Inside, he gropes around for candles and the box of long matches Merrill keeps on the hearth. It should be OK, the cops, armed forces, whatever are still all over at the lake, but he pulls the shades before he strikes the first match, in case. Her house is just the way he left it at dawn it seems like forever ago. God, is this really the same day?

Either Merrill went voluntarily or something took her so fast that she didn't have time to grab her phone or leave anything behind— a note, the bracelet he gave her, so he would know. Her cell is still on the dresser, but like the house phones and the phones in the other empty houses he'll try before he gives up on them entirely, it's dead. No signal, and no matter what he does, he can't find out whether the damn thing even recorded the dozen missed calls he made to her.

The silence is killing him. He tells the dog, "Dude, I bet you're hungry." He answers for the dog. "You bet I am." He does what he can for the grateful setter: he pours a box of Merrill's cornflakes into the biggest bowl he can find and sets it down for the dog. The dude slurps it up, tipping the bowl. Merrill's treasured raku is a dog dish now. *If she knew she's rip my ears off.* But Merrill doesn't know. He says, because Merrill isn't here to say the obvious, "There are a lot of things you don't know."

Don't whine!

He repeats, setting the words down like stones, "A lot of things."

Something about the darkness and silence, about the absolute Merrill-lessness of the house, of this kitchen, where they collided last night and left everything between them hanging. His lovely woman was *waiting,* and he totally missed the moment. Apparently, so did she: he finds her yukata on the floor by the rumpled bed. Abandoned slides. Naturally he mashes his face into her pillow. Yes, she was here. Yes she isn't, may never be. Either he sleeps or he doesn't. He couldn't tell you which. Davy hurls himself on the bed, thinking to crash just long enough to recharge, but he doesn't sleep. To his humiliation he plows through the bedding and presses Merrill's pillows to his face, rooting for that alien scent: Steele's shampoo, his shaving lotion, his living flesh, because his first instinct is to pin this on Rawson Steele.

Irrational? Probably. At this point Davy's a runaway train,

whirring along the track so fast that the next turn could derail him, but he won't slow down and he can't stop. The trouble with Merrill began the day Steele showed up, along with everything that's happened on Kraven since the slick intruder entered City Hall. Unless, Davy thinks. *Unless it started before he came.* Either the calculating bastard paid off everybody on Kraven island to disappear, he thinks, or he engineered this mass abduction to cover the fact that whatever it cost him, whatever it took to bring it off, he was going to have Merrill Lanieuville Poulnot, and he would do anything to cover the theft.

Yes, he is crazy with it.

No. Not crazy. Fact truth. Either Steele has stolen Davy's lover or he seduced her, that's for sure, and after hours of searching and wondering, he's too wrecked to know which would be worse.

Unless!

Fury drives him to his feet.

Standing in the middle of her bedroom in the damp early-morning air, shivering in Ray Powell's borrowed clothes, Davy is struck by the *unless.*

Terror keeps him there.

Unless Steele is . . . A shudder rips through him. Part of something bigger.

Where was he while I was stirring up chiggers at the Overlook, like redbugs would make an operator like Steele forget us and move on? What was he doing while I lay in wait for him out there on the breakwater, thinking I could manage and control the scene? What the fuck does he want?

Shit! Steele wants Merrill, whom he stupidly blew off in the middle of a major, decisive encounter that might have settled, that might have . . . oh God, if he'd only said . . . If he'd only done . . .

What? Whatever he has done or failed to do. A black hole opens in front of Davy, yawning, with Steele like a magnet at the bottom of the pit. Charming, sinister, calculating, so smooth and friendly, Rawson Steele is calling from the abyss: *come on down.*

What the fuck was he doing here?

Fuck, what am I doing here?

He grabs his LCD flash from the dresser. "Dude?" But the dog sprawls, rolling over onto Merrill's side of the bed, filling her space. It's so fucking depressing that he douses the flash and leaves the room, wandering in his mind.

Next he finds himself standing in the darkened kitchen with something nasty in his mouth, chewing without any idea how old this thing is or long it's been. He's reluctant to turn on his Maglite and see what he just ate. God, was he really gnawing on the half-eaten clam roll he threw in the fridge after the fight? So, what? Did the power go out the minute he rolled out of bed and left the house? He stumbles back to Merrill's bed, shoving the dog off Merrill's side, and crashes into sleep.

Stupid of him, dozing like he has forever, sleepwalking through the hours on the dumb premise that he's alone in the night. He thought the neighborhood was perfectly safe— shit, wasn't everybody down at the lake? No. Although the rows of houses were empty when he and the Dude came into this one, he's no longer alone. He can hear them coming down Poulnot Street: good old boys stomping along shouting in the dark. Police from Charlton and Poynter's island may be down at the lake, but cops and supernumeraries from wherever fanned out while he sat like a stalled cursor, going duh-duh-duh. There are slack-jawed bub- bas from wherever-the-fuck out there, stomping from house to house, kicking in doors, inspecting sheds and trashing houses in search of interlopers, bent on securing the crime scene.

If this is a crime scene.

The sky outside is turning pale. In an hour or so it will be light.

Davy snaps to. Where the bedroom was dark a minute ago, reflected dome lights and headlights play on the ceiling. While he was staring into the void, the official presence entered Poulnot Street. *Shit!* He rolls out of bed and lands in a crouch. They're next door, and they aren't exactly sneaking up. He can hear them crunching through the Clarsons' hedges and flower beds, trying to sound big.

Flashlights show in all the next-door windows, flickering from room to room in the deserted house. Guys he went to school with are out there rooting in the bushes with nightsticks, rifle barrels, whatever they had when they took up arms, stomping onto the porch baying like hounds to prove they're in charge. Armed thugs are working their way down Poulnot Street, and Merrill's house is next.

Still in a crouch, he gentles the dog back onto the bed and rolls him over. "Dude," he murmurs, scratching the soft belly, "you have to stay back, or they'll get you. You be good," he says and then adds, without conviction, "And I'll be back."

14

Ned

Argh!

It's after midnight and dark as fuck in here; my room is sealed— airless, like a coffin sealed to keep death from getting out, but *something got in*. I can hear it breathing.

Trapped in this fucking desert city and locked down for the night, I am not alone. My hole in the wall behind the dumb-waiter is way too tight for anybody but me, so, who? Like, how? Father's on guard 24/7, but even with the house secured and the Great Poulnot crouched in the front room like the troll under a drawbridge, holy crap, something got into my room!

What. What?

I rise up and burp words at it. "What?"

"Shut up."

All the lights here go on all at once, and, *fuck!* Rawson Steele is in my room, not-quite whistling. "How did you get in?"

He talks with his mouth clamped tight, so only you can hear. "I said. Shut. The fuck. Up."

I can't help it, I go, "Boy, am I glad to see you!"

He doesn't look all that glad to see me. "My fucking phone."

"Like I've got it?" Yes I am pissed off at him.

"Asshole, keep it down."

"What do you think, I stole it?"

"Don't yell! The old man will . . ."

Why do I not tell him Father won't *whatever* because he can't? Because I don't know what Father can and can't do, I only know what he's done, that keeps me locked up tight and crazy. That's the whole thing about Father. Even when you think you know what he's doing, you never really know. I whisper, "What do you want?"

"My fucking phone."

"Why? It's not like anything is working."

"We're getting it back. In case."

"We?" Cool. He thinks this is a *we* situation. Like we're friends. I go, "What's the point? It's not like you can get a signal in this place."

"It's urgent." The angles in his face are sharper than I thought. Like, he could be one of the Koro Ishi in *Gaijin Samurai*, maybe Takeda, who I always thought was the strongest player on my team— smart, probably a lot older than us. Unless— oh shit, what if he's the power behind the Dread Kobyashi, our enemy from the first level all the way to the top? Like, should I trust this guy and fall in line or sneak up behind him and nail him or what? I am back in the game and I come at him all Hydra Destroyer, beady-eyed and snarling through my teeth. "What makes you think you can even get a call?"

He tosses a stinking bundle at me. Yesterday's scrubs. "Dress."

"Wait. Who's calling who?"

"Now." His glare strips the Hydra Destroyer off me like flaking paint.

And like plain old ordinary Ned Poulnot, dumb baby following orders because Father says, I put them on, but I'm all, "OK, how are you gonna take a call or make one or even text anybody in this dead bone place?" I can't stop jabbering. "Even the pagers died."

His eyes rake me raw. "Don't ask."

So I don't. I just stand there wishing Father would come— what am I thinking? *Wait.* I don't wish Father would come, I wish Father would . . . I don't know what I wish. I wish Rawson Steele wasn't so much bigger than me, I wish he wasn't so ripped and tough and driven, and I wish he'd . . .

I wish I didn't feel so short and stupid and useless standing here in paper shoes and yesterday's dirty scrubs.

Then he truly scares the crap out of me. It's the cold, dead lead in his voice. That death-row stare. Like he really is the player that runs Kobyashi in the game and this is a new level that I don't know about. He waves me out of the room. "Move!"

"*Gaijin Samurai*," I say anyway. He's either my friend or my enemy and I kind of need to know.

He doesn't blink. "Are you coming or not?"

"Are you with me or against me?" I toss it out there, to make sure he's only pretending we aren't in the game. "Like, at Chinyatsu Yo?"

Something makes me look again: Takeda? Did the player behind Takeda step out of the game to help me escape? I ask, to make sure. "Do you care?"

"Not really." That grin. It's something about the grin.

"So, what. Are we in this thing together?"

Then he really grins.

It's Takeda! It has to be. I go, "So, we're in this together?"

Shit, we can change whatever's going down in this weird white place, him and me, fighting back to back no matter what.

He doesn't rightly say. He just says, "OK then. Let's go."

Truth? I would follow him anywhere, but I want him to think I'm too sharp to move just because he says so. "Where to?"

"Where do you think, stupid? Your sister's house."

"She took your phone?"

"That guy Powell did. I saw him hand it off to her on their way out to the rim."

"The rim?" He might as well be talking about another planet.

"Take these." He throws another bundle at me. Wow, a black hoodie so I can streak around and vanish into the night like Rawson Steele. Black sweats, where does he get these things? "It's cold out, and farther than you think."

I slide into my disguise and follow him out into the hall. He doesn't need to tell me to be quiet, we are, oh my God, we're heading for the front door, with Father planted at the table like a stone idol of himself, propping up that big head with his fists. He's been stuck in that position, rooted in one place for so long that his elbows have turned black. The beard is so white that you can see the skin showing through, and his chin is all black and blue, like all the blood in him sank to the bottom and my father is morphing into a gigantic bruise. It spooks the crap out of me and I accidentally bump the corner of his table just when I'm trying so hard to sneak. "Shit!" *Oh, shit.*

Oh, holy crap.

No problem. He doesn't move. Only the head comes to life. He raises it like a sea monster, waking up, with long white hair streaming over his eyes and that beard streaming down onto his chest like he just surfaced, with the whole ocean dripping down his face. His mouth opens wide under all that hair, as if he's trying to say something important but can't get it out because he's drowning in time and, fuck! I really don't care.

Then it all comes in on me: what Father is like, what it's been like with him, all of it, the parts in my soul that hurt all the time and the outside parts that he hurt but never so you'd see a scar or a broken bone or anything to prove it. *Hampton fucking Poulnot, I am done with you,* so I look him dead in the eyes, or where I think his eyes are under all that hair.

He might be trying to speak.

Like I even care. I shrug him off and tramp on by and out of his house here and on Kraven island and anywhere else in the universe. I'm gone from this place and out of his life in this or any other kingdom, I am done with Father for good and all.

I'm with Takeda now, although that may not be who he really is. Me and Rawson Steele are joining together to fight our way out of this dead hole and back to freedom, wherever that turns out to be, but still, but still . . .

It's weird.

Our front door is standing wide open to the night, which makes me feel both better and worse about how Rawson Steele got in, so that's Thing One.

Did he pick the locks or does this mean that he is secretly one of Them and They let him in Father's house to, like, do Their bidding, whoever *They* are?

That's Thing Two, and this is Thing Three: at this point, nobody from Kraven even knows whether there is a *They*. There's no way of telling how many more Things I have to keep track of, or whether I'll ever run out of Things that creep me out.

Thing Four is another *whether.*

I don't know how long it's been since we got dumped in this awful place, but fuck, I'm sick of not doing anything and not going anywhere, all trapped inside with the man . . .

OK, the man I hate most in this or any other universe.

Just then Father raises his arms to me; he could even be pleading, and that does it. I'm out of here. Takeda or Rawson Steele or tool of the dead white city, I could care less who I'm following into the freezing night.

My main man came and cracked me out, like, a minute and a half before I totally lost it and murdered Father and the Power went *Zot* or whatever and I turned to stone. Scientists would dig us up a million years from now, Hydra Destroyer like a marble chess piece and his stony father propped up at that table forever, monuments to some unknown thing that nobody cares about.

The cold air zaps me in the face. It's so cold out that everything I was thinking, including all the *whethers,* blows clean out of my head. It's like being unshelled, turned loose in the universe without a clue. Fuck Rawson Steele! He doesn't treat me like we're in this together. Not now that we're outside. He doesn't say X or Y to me, you know, instructions; he doesn't, like, send up flags, you know: *this way,* to make me think he actually gives a crap if I follow or not. He just takes off and I light out after him. We're on the run!

I squeeze out "Wait up," but it's too little and too late for him to hear. He's running along so far ahead that I have to drop into a crouch and go tearing after him, following him by ear, that fucking song that he's whistling through his teeth.

Together we cross the white city, me and the night stalker, leaning into the wind. The two of us run along like rats, streaking between the rows of Monopoly-board houses and down the creepy alleyways that take us along behind, avoiding the checkerboard spots where blinding streetlights mark off squares of night. We rush across the blank face of Wherever This Is under that totally fake full moon, tearing along like Steele knows where he's going, and I wonder if we'll ever get to Merrill's house or if we are going to someplace better or different or, OK, worse.

We run until a stitch stabs me in the ribs. I yelp and bend double but he doesn't look back and I don't know how to get home from where we are. No way am I stopping now. I just follow the tune, sticking close enough to see which turn he'll take next, but every time I make a corner, cramping like to die, shit! He heads around the next. Then just when I see a chance to catch up, he pulls a hard right.

I want to yell loud enough to bring Them down on us, **Wait!** But he trusts me— I think.

He needs me, right? I rear up on my hind legs like a crippled centipede and follow, so crazy with keeping up that when he finally stops, I run up his heels like the biggest, dumbest kid in Special Ed.

"Ow!" He whirls with his teeth bared and his eyes blazing. "Watch it!"

My face goes to pieces, like, down around my neck. *I thought we were friends.* "Sorry."

"OK then." He slams my shoulders with the heel of his hand and spins me around like this is urgent and I should know.

We are standing in front of another blank white house.

Shit, he marches me up the walk like a lead soldier, his right foot and left foot shoving mine, *right, left, right. March. Hup. Two*— what was he before we got dumped in this desert, Special Ops?

I dig in. Like, What is this? Where are we, and why me? *Any-thing* could be behind that door. "What's this about?"

"You'll see." He's like steel, marching me the distance that I don't want to go. *Reep. Fo.* We stop just short of the pool of light on the front stoop. He points.

Except for the peephole, the front door looks just like Fa-ther's, like all the other front doors out here. *"What do you want me to do?"*

He bends, harshing into my ear. "When she comes to the peep-hole, smile." Then he shoves me into the light.

It's kind of awful. It's so bright, the door is so just like every other door that I don't get what I'm supposed to know. Where this is. Why I'm here. My friend Rawson and me, we ran all the way across the floor of crazy Wherever to get to this dead white house that I don't know whose it is or whether he's still my friend or why this is so important.

"This is where I owe you a big one." He's all, like, *man to man.* Then he grins. "She'll open up for you."

"Oh," I say. I get it. "Oh."

I'm stopped stone dead and shivering outside my sister's house. The phone. We're here about his stupid phone and I'm scared shit that after all this, like it's the wrong house and we get busted, or else it's the right one, but she isn't home. Or she won't let me in. Unless it's a trap. They'll come to the door all right, but it won't be her, it's the devil or the Merganauts from *Gaijin Samurai,* fixing to drag me and Steele or Takeda and my whole team Koro Ishi straight to hell.

"Be cool," he says. "I've got your back."

I push the buzzer and nothing happens. I knock and nobody comes. I lean down and whistle two notes into the keyhole, like Mom used to whistle when it was OK for us to come out of our rooms for supper, never mind what Father just did to her. That should bring her. If that won't do it, nothing will. Next to me, hanging in the shadows just outside the halogen glare, Rawson Steele waits it out, all intense and jittering.

I call in the lowest tone you can use and actually call to a person. "Merrill, are you in there?" What if she is? What if she's not? If I bang on the door and yell and that doesn't get to her, then maybe at least It or They will come out and grab us so this can end.

That would be something, right?

Right?

I ball up my fists and bang hard enough to bring out the dead or bring down the walls of Wherever This Is, and I hate that the fucking place doesn't even have a fucking name. "I know you're in there, Merrill Poulnot. Open the door, Mer. Answer the fucking door, I'm your fucking brother. Hurry up, Merrill Laneuville Poulnot. It's me."

And she opens it so fast and whips me inside so slickly and slams it so hard that without Rawson Steele's knife— his knife!— laid in the crack it would have locked, but my big sister is hugging me so hard that she doesn't even know it hurts. She's all sobby and going, "Are you OK? What were you thinking, Ned Poulnot, you could have died running around out there in the cold, you could get hurt, or killed, oh God, Neddy, I'm so sorry I had to leave you behind," she says, and I don't know if she means now or back then when she was eighteen, but I know she gets it; she gets me, and she's sorry as all hell.

"The thing is, I had to, we had to . . . And we're stuck in the houses where they put us, so it's you and Father all over again, but he's too far gone to hurt anybody now. Listen, when we get home . . ." She hugs me again. "Hey, I'm working on it. Ray and I have . . ." This is not making sense. Then it is. "It's just taking too long!"

And, fuck, we don't either of us know if it's been days or weeks.

"We're trying," my sister says, "and we still don't know. We don't know anything!" Then she buries my face in her belly and starts hugging and rocking, and whether or not she knows that Rawson Steele has blown into the room like a spirit on the wind, she's crying to break my heart, "Oh, Neddy, I missed you so much!"

15

Hampton Poulnot

> When I die, reduce me to ash
> dig out the gold, it's worth hard cash
> kick the rest out the door, baptize it with pee
> I know what you think of me

Damn you, Dorcas Lanieuville, I wrote verse to please you, and now look. I loved you to hell, and you threw out generations of history like yesterday's dead fish. You were bent on tearing down the family tree, so you called our daughter Merrill, ridiculous made-up name. I tried to forgive you, I did. "It means bright as the sea," you said, putting your stamp on my baby like a curse. We tried, but you vanished from my life like a spirit on the wind, and that, I will never forgive. Now your righteous daughter and uptight Ray Powell— well, God damn you all.

On Kraven, I was a leader! Ray Powell was my *friend*. Time passed. I drank and you ran and forgive me, I drank. I drank and worse things happened. I lost my temper all over again. Ray Powell turned my people against me; he did it with that smile, extorting promises I couldn't keep, so he took me off the bench. *For your own good,* he said when he brought me down, but that's not what he meant. *He stole my power,* but now.

Listen, our Creator lifted me up! No prophecies this time, no burning bush to signify change. It just happened.

We woke up here, set out like chess pieces on a white board without markings, shuddering in the murderous heat. I took it as a sign. My people delivered to me, diminished by the glare. Helpless and terrified, they turned to me. *At last.*

For their sake, I raged at the elements. I ran; I thought they would follow as I cried to heaven, *Explain!* They were poised to follow me anywhere. The great screen overhead came to life, and like dumb animals they turned away from me, looking for answers up there on the screen.

We watched and watched, but there were no answers up there, just TV.

Now, we Poulnots ruled on Kraven island for too long for Hampton Poulnot IV to give up. Delroy Root stood by me; he was weeping. I seized on him and climbed, and he was glad. I rose up like Gabriel, trumpeting, **Explain!** We ran like angels, **Explain,** and in that one perfect moment all of Kraven island united behind me, even Ray Powell, every one of us bawling, "*Explain.*"

I had the power; it was magnificent. I thought, *This is my time.* Until the unknown entity moved its huge hand. Overhead, the pictures died. Then, God! *My people* turned on me! Me, the new Moses, *this close* to leading them out of the desert.

They blamed me.

My people dragged me down. They fell on me like jackals and then, help me, help me Jesus. It wasn't God, intervening. It was Ray Powell. He rose up all sacred and holy like the saints and popes, Ray Powell and Dorcas— **Where did that come from? No!**

He and Merrill, *your daughter,* carried me away before I could . . . **Dorcas? Is that you?**

What were you up to all those years ago, you and sanctimonious Ray Powell, so grand. Kind, you told me the night before you left, so kind, were you meeting in some big city, planning our ruination?

Do you know what's happened? Do you even care?

Powell and that ingrate Merrill brought me to this white egg crate of a house, along with your perfidious son. My daughter and my best friend. Well, God. Damn. Them.

You will rot in hell for this you . . . *Dorcas,* and it will serve you right. At the door to this white hell, you . . . Merrill! You told your baby brother, that *child,* "Keep an eye on him," and shoved us inside. *Imperious,* with your "Ned will take care of you," and then— as if I'd forgotten!— Powell put both hands on my shoulders, "You need time to regroup," and pushed me backward into this room, saying exactly what he said last time, *It's for your own good.*

You said it with that same monstrous, kindly smile you smiled when you forced me out of the courthouse, Ray Powell. Like a father distracting a child with a little toy, you added, "You have a book to write," you righteous prick.

Now the boy is gone, he waltzed out with that stalking dagger Rawson Steele; the man tweaked my hair as though I'd ceased to exist.

Well, I'll show you.

THINGS TO DO

First: gather forces to find and confront the authorities here, and I will do it, but first!

A. Regain control. Let my people dispose of Ray Powell.

No! **First:**

A. Regain my people's trust. They must follow without question.

    a. Make them see every God. Damned. Thing I did for them, so they'll keep the faith!

It was Ray Powell who turned my people against me. Ray Powell shut me inside this box and locked me in, and they won't come and they don't send messages and they never visit, not even Merrill. The image of her mother and . . . Don't. b. What's b?

b. Make a Plan and lay it out for them, so they'll stop thinking what they're thinking and believe in me again.
Second:

Thank God the boy is gone, he and that sleek weasel; he came slinking into our town just before, *what was he doing there, why is he here—* he and my ungrateful little . . .
Et tu, motherfucker, the next time I lay hands on you . . .
I saw you leaving, Edward LaMar Poulnot, you and your friend the Antichrist. You cheeky bastard, you didn't even bother to sneak, but if you think I don't have the power to stop you, then God damn your eyes. You didn't escape. I let you go. It was a conscious decision, and I am damn glad to get shut of you. I need the space, and now. Now . . .

When I die, and you turn me to ash . . .

Stop that! No verse, not now, not when I . . .

Second . . .

Dear God, I don't know what *Second* is.
Understand, I am Hampton Calhoun Poulnot of the Poulnot family out of Charleston and Kraven island and nobody takes

that away from me! I will go forth, and my people will rise up! With my people at my back I will find Ray Powell and lock Ray Powell in this antiseptic cell and see how he likes it. Then my people and I will march out and get Them or It or He who extracted us and dumped us here, we will get *out* of this place and I will get even, no matter who or what I have to destroy.

Although this is no Egypt and much is uncertain, I am, by God, their leader, and if I need to prove it all over again, I will. Without distractions, without the incessant chatter of the boy, badgering, cajoling, threatening me:— Eat this, Father.— Father, do that!— Father, can I . . .

Like Moses, I need solitude to think.

When I die, reduce me to ash . . .

Agh! Where did that come from? Dorcas, poetry I used to write for you, for all the good that did. Now, go away. Like Moses in the desert, I know my time has come, but unlike Moses, I don't have forty years! Are my people unfaithful? Were you? *Leave me alone!*

Stop. We were put here in the great white nothing for a purpose, and I *will not move* until I have divined it.

You who put me here, listen!

I was in charge! Now look. Moses and his people made it out of the desert by the grace of God, but if Ray Powell could bring me down, who's to say whether or not there is a God, or whether He caused this or if He is watching or whose side He is on, and if He or It or They. . . .

Don't! About the explanations, there will be no explanations. Focus on the plan.

My list. Must. Make. List.

First *No.* **Second . . .**

And once it's done, sift my ashes for gold . . .

Damn you, damnable, mealymouthed, shiteating *verse* drifting in like the perfume in the handkerchief that Dorcas left behind. His people complained but they followed Moses, unlike my egregious, whining malcontents.

Every great leader has moments of doubt, but this . . .

Look at us, honest Carolinians all, born of good families, set down in the desert like so many objects, rearranged to please the eye. Unless we're livestock, waiting for the the butcher's axe.

God it's quiet. Guilt rushes in to fill the space.

When I die, sift my ashes for gold.
No, forgiveness can't be bought or sold . . .

Dorcas, not now, I have things to do. But at this great distance, *after all this time,* certain *things I did* rise up and congeal in my throat: the past lodges like a clot— can't cough it up, can't make it go down. Must think, I have to *think,* but you entered the space like an invading army, filling me with . . . If I knew, I would put it away, but vengeful God, you have raised Dorcas Lanieuville, and I can't.

. . . but gold pulled from ash can be melted down

"Don't!"

What do you want from me, Dorcas? Presents, after all the presents you refused? Apologies? Why should I apologize? You're the one who ran out on us. After everything I did for you.

God I need a drink.

Even Moses had bad days, right?

Every leader was young once, idealistic, full of hope. I came back to the island from Clemson and two years in the Army, three in law school, and in time, my people made me a judge and I was happy, up to a point. I met Dorcas one night in Savannah— so pretty, but we in the Carolinas come out of a great tradition, and her people didn't *do* like we do. Still, I went back to see Dorcas again and again; she was so lovely and so needy, we loved each other so much.

I rescued her from her sordid life. Voodoo white-trash family, squatting in the Savannah salt marsh; their kind goes in and out with the tides, but my Dorcas rose up out of the mud all glowing and lovely. I brought her home to Kraven, and then. Oh, then . . . I'm sorry you made me mad, but . . . I gave you Mama's diamonds to make up for it, and that other time, I gave you the Calhoun coin silver because I couldn't erase the scar and you know I loved you *so much*. Never mind what we said to each other that first time or what came between us or what I did to her later, when I was drunk. You were wrong to leave my offerings behind when you ran, but you.

It was the pressure. The demands on a great leader are tremendous. You may control your people, but you can't curb their wants. Blame the pressure of their expectations, Dorcas. It's huge! Could you not grant me that? Was it that bad between us, certain things I said or did to you? It was an accident! Some, I still remember. Most, I'd rather not, but you have to understand. A leader is a force of nature, like God. In hurricanes, when the eye crosses our island the air is still, but the wind will come, and when that 'cane roars back in on you, there's no stopping what comes next.

So wrong.

Woman, what do you want from me? I carried the weight of

all Kraven on my shoulders. Their wants. No, their *needs* bored into the living heart of me, and if I snapped in your presence and let it all fly, you know I loved you, and you must have known why. So what if I drank to relax and sometimes I flew off, I'll never forgive you for taking our problems out of the house.

That night I followed you to his office, you were in there past midnight, conspiring! I didn't ask and you never said, but I know. And what were you and he doing on all those other nights when you left my house in tears, what were you doing anyway?

Second . . .

"Bitch, what do you want from me!"
Things you should have said and never said.

When I die, if the things I said . . .

Dear God, here I am with all our lives and safety at risk, with all our futures in my hands, and I'm hung up on a God. Damned. Poem. This is what failure does to you. Can't talk, can't argue, can't get out to raise my army, I can't even finish this wretched to-do list.

Instead I sit here pushing words around as though, as soon as they march in order, I can get her back, no. As though I can make certain corrections and move on. OK, woman! I'll do this thing, and then, and then . . .

When I die, sift my ashes for gold.
No, forgiveness can't be bought or sold
but gold pulled from ash can be melted down
to a medal or a golden crown.

The best I can do, after years of shit.
You were wise to run away from it.

Hours here, and this is all I have? Oh God. Woman, I have responsibilities! So much to do, so many things standing in my way and now, you, whole in spite of certain things I did to you, Dorcas, you're back again, too big for the space.

You do what you have to, to get things done.

I lived in the hour, but Dorcas foresaw. The woman knew what I would become without her to stand between me and her young, but the woman left me— was I that bad, that she vanished with no warning and without explanation? Did she not care what happened to them?

Winds destroy, survivors float
Unfaithful women drown and bloat.

The bitch didn't even leave a note.

16

Merrill
Now

Ned comes in, and night and silence blow out the door. After years spent battling Father, after a string of so-so roommates, after all the joy and confusion that came with Davy moving in, I was getting used to coming home to peace and order. I like walking into silence, everything where I left it, nothing to do, nobody expecting anything.

Now my still, featureless house is filling up with need.

Neddy slams into me and locks his arms so tight that I gasp. Clamping me in that hug, he twirls us so my back is to the door. I know he's hiding something, but I'm so glad to see him that I let it play. We're spinning in the moment, Neddy and me, all, *not yet, make it last, it's been too long!* I could swear he's grown. He's so strong that I have to run my fingers up under the baggy hoodie and drum on his ribs to make him giggle and let go.

He smells like my brother but he doesn't; I catch subtle hints of, what. Men's deodorant and motor oil and— wait. One other thing. Oh! I get it, but I don't want to.

I hold him off so I can study him. Instead of acknowledging the man poised on the sill, neither outside nor in, I draw on recent history. "You were smoking weed."

"As if!"

So much for assumptions. This is not his shirt. Everything we thought before here— before *this place*— is long gone.

The intruder speaks. "In your dreams, lady. Hello again."

Yes, this is what I have been avoiding. Magnetic, in spite of everything that stands between us. *You're not that person now, leave her back in high school, you're done yearning after guys you know are bad for you.* "What are you, stalking me?"

Black sweats, black hoodie, same as Ned's, but it looks better on him because it fits. Look at him, lounging in my doorway with one foot propped on the frame, studying his buffed fingernails as though whatever he came for, whatever he wants from me, can wait. He takes his sweet time responding and when he does, it's to piss me off. "You don't like me, do you?"

"I don't know you!"

Rawson Steele backs into my open door, shuts it with one hand and shoots the bolt without looking, as if he knows these buildings by heart. "My point."

"What?" I ask him, "What do you want from us?"

"What do you think I want?"

Right. The phone. When we rounded that corner tonight the phone was still spinning in the road but the owner was long gone. "So that was you."

This makes him laugh, but his mouth twitches and I wonder: feeling stupid because you dropped it? About running away when it was only me and Ray? Embarrassed grin. "Pretty much."

"You were out of there too fast. Who knew? It's not like we could give it back."

"It's not like you wanted to. Now, if you'll just . . ."

The minute Ray scooped up that phone I flipped it open. Its screen was shattered but there was a voice coming out. *Expected more from you*; that flawless, automated tone threw me into a fit of speculation. *Waiting for your . . .* Then it died and no matter how hard we shook it, that was all we got.

Ray mouthed, Oh. My. God. I nodded. Yes.

My needy intruder's phone is useless, but I'm not about to let him know that. "Not yet."

He smiles. Nicely, as though this isn't really an issue for him. "Is there a problem?"

Shrug like you don't care. I turn away, playing for time. "Give me a minute." I go into the bedroom to think. Ray handed the phone off to me as though through some miracle I'd bring it back to life or shake the owner's secrets out of it. No way.

Maybe I can use it to shake some secrets out of him.

I pull the high-end phone with all its broken bells and whistles out from under the mattress and write my opening speech before I open the bedroom door. You'd think I'd walked in on them. The Northerner and my kid brother have their heads together: partners in collusion, laughing like old friends. Something snaps and the speech that I planned to hold until I caught him off-guard roars to the top.

"What were you doing out in my backyard?"

It surprises both of us but he recovers with a surprisingly sweet grin. "What makes you think it was me?"

"I saw you out there the night before the . . ." Disruption? Outrage? I can't find the noun. I can't shake the memory either.

We were together on my front porch that weird last night on Kraven island; he lingered, and I didn't mind; he was vibrant, edgy, attractive, compelled by a need he wouldn't get time to name. We were poised at the edge of something, I'm not sure what, but for the first time in forever, I caught that old high school vibe: *so not good for you. So . . . don't go there, girl.*

Clearly, it was urgent: "story I have to tell you . . ." implied, *story I alone am left to tell.*

Just then Davy pulled in. When I turned back to draw out the rest, he was gone. Davy was shitty about it, me with the devil/destroyer, which precipitated that fight in my kitchen in the dead of night.

"Why was he here?"

I was furious because I didn't know!

He pressed. "What *was* that?"

I fobbed him off with a pat TV line: "Who *are* you?"

"I'm your . . ." He couldn't find a word! Five years and nothing between us to seal the deal, the jerk. I slapped takeout cartons on the table so we wouldn't have to fight, but I was fuming. Too disrupted by things I wish I'd said to sleep. Some time after midnight the two of us collided in the dark, Davy foraging, me too distracted to rest, the real problem pending. I put it to him and we had the fight.

On my way back to bed I thought I caught the glint of a shovel out there underneath the moon, a figure working— *what was that?* At the time I thought, *Tell Davy in the morning.* I thought we would wake up together and sort ourselves out. That night the last thing I said to him in the kitchen was, "If you're that kind of possessive, it's time to put up or shut up." He walked away. I didn't know that was the last thing I would ever say to him. I saw somebody in our backyard and I thought, *It can damn well wait 'til tomorrow. It serves you right,* but by morning we were all . . .

Oh crap, there's no noun for what we all were, all of us all at once.

But Rawson Steele is waiting so I start over. "The night before the . . ." The word comes, and I explode. ". . . Removal!"

"Is that what you think it was?" His eyes are clear blue and, this is odd: bottomless. Impossible to plumb. "A removal?"

"I don't know what to think!"

The Northerner came to Kraven island and caught us unawares. He made friends fast, and he did it without explaining what he was doing here on the Inland Waterway. He had that kind of charm. Nice way about him, soft-spoken, strong handshake, black raw silk shirt, open collar, because everyone knows that for such encounters, you show your throat to let the people know you are in their hands, not the other way around.

Ray brought him into my office that first day. "Merrill, this is Rawson Steele."

All he had to do was smile. Chiseled head, but with that smile, and a disarming nick in one of those perfect front teeth. Here researching the "colony," he told me: finding out about all old families and why Azalea House was the only plantation house left standing. He just wanted to walk the land where the other plantations stood, outlining the tabby foundations of the ruined houses, he wanted to lie down in the remains of the slave quarters and listen to the heart of the island life; he said he needed to find out, but he never said what.

He was on fire with it, so in love with our island that he couldn't seem to find the words, and I thought, *Sweet.* I liked him at once— we all did— well, everybody but Davy, and to this day I don't know if it was instinct or plain old sexual jealousy, but to my shame I worked it. I did, because Davy and I were at a confusing time in our lives together and I thought . . . Never mind what I thought. *He wasn't coming out of the house when you found him on our front porch that night, Davy, he just dropped by.*

If you care.

On his second day in town he came into my office with that

great smile. "I'm scouting locations for a documentary on your island and I need your help." His face was bright with whatever he hoped for, but he never quite said what we have on Kraven island that he is so desperate to have.

No. What we had.

I walked him along Bay Street in Kraventown, pointing out this, explaining that. At Ray's party I introduced him around. He's a magnet; people liked him, what can I say? *Still do.* It's exciting seeing him here, but. God, I am uneasy.

We let him into our lives because in the tidelands, generations survive on the persistence of good manners. We all make nice to strangers because in our part of the world, you do. We let him into our stores and offices, our houses. We let him into our lives, and now look at us.

Here.

I saw you digging in the dirt behind my house the night before it happened. Or not, and I don't know which.

He fills my bleak living room, all arrogant and handsome and borderline sinister, grinning like the fox sizing up the chickens that invited him in. Prompting me: "You were saying . . ."

I jerk to, jittering. Embarrassed, because parts of me just came alive. *How long has it been?* "Nothing. I was just." It's a sentence I can't finish, not right now.

He says patiently, "You called this— whatever, this *phenomenon* that picked us all up and dropped us here— The Removal. What did you mean?"

"What do you mean, us?" *Is that really me screeching?* The noise shames even me. "You ought to know . . ."

His eyebrows shoot up— surprise? "Shhh, don't yell."

Furious, I let him have it. ". . . You fucking caused it!"

"Is that what you think?" Yes, he is surprised.

"You bet I do! All this stuff you have, that we don't." I try to clarify. "Black sweats, the hoodie. Those boots. This phone." I throw it at his head. "You were talking to Them."

"No." Instead of ducking he catches the phone and turns it over, flashing its ruined face. "Shit. Busted."

"Just the screen. It was working when we found it."

"Nope." *Oh, man. Please don't smile!* "Nothing works here."

"Then why are you so crazy to get it back?"

"Personal reasons."

"I heard that voice." . . . *acknowledge. If you can't talk, press 1 to signify* . . . an automated voice, but I could swear I heard other voices rising behind it.

He continues, "Urgent ones."

Helpful Ned says, "Rush call."

"You only think you heard it."

"Them. In the background, talking to you."

"Oh," he says; he's so damn smooth. "You mean the recording." He taps the phone the way you do when you can't believe your pet has died on you. Is that a sigh? He shrugs. "It was just a recording."

If I persist he'll just deny it, so I attack. "Then why are you so crazy to get it back?"

"It's personal."

Apologetic grin, but I don't quit. "And where were you on the day they dumped everybody else in one spot, and what have you been doing out there? Where were you anyway? At some kind of headquarters that we don't know about? Like, reporting to Them?"

"There is no Them."

"Fuck yes there is. Unless you . . ." *Shit!* I stab the air. "You. You did this to us."

Ned's elbow clips me in the ribs. "The hell he did!"

"Not now, Ned."

"Look," Steele says. "If I brought us here, don't you think I would get us the hell out of here?"

"I don't know what you would do!"

"I'm *trying*!" He reaches for my hands.

"Let go!"

Ned goes, "Mer . . ."

"Look at me." His lean face is taut. When we are nose to nose, he lets go unexpectedly and backs away with his hands spread— a living signboard that reads: TRUST ME. "I don't know either."

"Merrill . . ."

"I *said,* not now!" Even now I am neither here nor there about Rawson Steele. I don't know who he is or what he really wants, what he's doing here or what we're doing here or what to do about it, I don't *know,* any more than I know what's going to become of us. We are in stasis here until the wire holding me in place snaps and I attack. "Like hell you don't! You caused this. You can damn well get us out of it."

"MER!"

"Love to, but I can't." Rawson Steele fixes me with his eyes. I look deep. The irises are green at the center, and as empty as ponds. "I told you, I don't know shit."

Then the kid— *my brother*— cuts between us, spitting like a panther. "FUCK YES HE DOES. I SAW HIM."

I wheel on my brother, pleading, "For God's sake, Neddy, don't yell!"

But there is no silencing Ned. "HE GOES OUTSIDE THE RIM, MERRILL. I KNOW IT. I SAW HIM COMING IN."

17

Davy
Friday, near dawn

It's eerie, slinking through his adopted home town like an alien presence— with a third eye, furry antlers, he doesn't know, just that he is different here— unless he's a clumsy spy from some foreign country we didn't know we were at war with. The feeling is strange and terrible. He thought he could make a home here, but flushed out of Merrill's house by good old boys with down-home drawls, lunging from hedge to garbage bin for cover, he no longer belongs.

In spite of the commotion on Poulnot Street, all the lights on the Kraven island grid are dead. What's left comes from other sources. Emergency LEDs set up at the roadblock signify a police presence. One state trooper patrols with his fog lights on, one cop paces back and forth along Bay Street with a pencil flash while the others are, what? Fanning out in Ray's neighborhood? Still out at the lake, waiting? Waiting for what?

Empty police cars and the TV truck stand ready to roll into action, but when?

They were sounding the lake when he went into Merrill's house, but it's been a while. Are they still dragging or did they find something? Drowned sailors rising out of the disrupted waters, he thinks, or putrid swamp things, dripping with underwater growths.

Hideous images come up out of the mud at the bottom of his mind. Stop that. Be cool. They're still waiting to see whether bodies float up because no bodies have floated up, which means everybody from Kraven is somewhere else and Merrill's fine.

Unless they're done dragging and they're waiting to see what the divers bring up. Abandoned cars or the skeletons of ancient suicides or the bodies of his best friend on Kraven and his angry lover. Who?

A cold, wet nose grazes his wrist and he reaches out. *You followed me!* Touched, he sets his hand on the dog's bony head, and feels its whole body shivering with love. Yes, Ray's dog slipped off the bed and came running out into the night to look after him. *Oh Dude,* he thinks, but can't bring himself to say. *Oh, Dude.* Quick and furtive, he keeps to the shadows, scared of being seen and scared nobody will see him because without him knowing it had happened or how it happened, David Ribault of Charlton, Yale and the offshore islands no longer exists.

It makes this not better, but *easier,* knowing the Dude is walking point. *When Ray comes back I'll tell him this is the dog's real name.* Running ahead of the darkness, he pins his heart on the return in spite of the shuttered store windows lining Bay Street, the gaping jaws of the Episcopal church, everything in this town dead empty. Deserted. Apt analogy for David Ribault's soul. At least the dog. *Oh, Dude.*

It's odd. The back door to Weisbuch's store is open— guess this event, this kidnapping or vanishment, this *whatever it was* caught Marlon out back. Right. Randolph Flatley would have come in with the first catch of the day, but that was hours ago. Randolph's truck smells pretty high, and whatever Marlon was buying is rotting in the road. The Dude is pretty excited. Davy grabs his collar and wrestles him away from the dead fish and into the deserted store, growling, "Dude, don't! It'll make you sick."

Then, what? *What?* A voice comes back at him from somewhere below. Flat. Dull. *Whut.* "Whut, Dave? Dave, whut done it?"

"Holy crap, Boogie, is that you?"

When he got out of the hospital after the botched adenoid surgery, Marlon Weisbuch made a place for Boogie at the back of his store. When they saw that the damage could not be fixed, Marlon fixed up a sweet room for Boogie in the basement—pine paneling, Barcalounger and bath, all that. Now his big, confused friend's voice comes upstairs ahead of him. "How did I get this way?"

Davy's flash lights up that round, empty face. "The operation, Boog, remember?"

Boogie wails, *"That's not what I mean."*

"Shh, Boogie, it's all over cops out there. When did you get back?"

"Back?"

"Back from Poyntertown, Thibault's creek, wherever you were when it came down." *Went up?*

"Never went nowhere. Been here."

"Like, before it happened?"

"I done tole you." Boogie's voice spikes. "I been here!"

Easy, don't start him caterwauling. "You saw it?"

Boogie gulps down a sob. "Almost."

"What do you mean, almost?"

"Everything shook, the world, my bed. It shook so hard I put the pillow over my head and hunkered down."

You're supposed to go easy with Boogie because he's different now, take it slow to match his pace, but Davy's wound so tight that he seizes Boogie by the wrist. "Now, why would you do that?"

"Ow!"

"Oh crap, Boog, I'm sorry. I didn't mean to." He pats the hurt place on Boogie like a mom curing an imaginary cut.

The sob explodes. "I was *so scared*. I hid under the bed."

Davy tries to gentle him with a sweet, mom voice. "It's OK, Boog, it's OK, everybody's scared."

"You don't get it. God come for 'em, but I was hiding! Time I come outside, they was gone and it flashed green."

"What did?"

"In the sky. Don't you get it? They was raptured up." He shakes his head and big tears fly. "God come down and I was hiding!"

With an effort, Davy pares the hard edge off his voice and comes in nicer, as close as he can get to soft. "Oh shit, Boogie, don't cry."

Too late. He wails, "God took everybody but me."

So they stand there in the dark not knowing. He can't comfort Boogie but he does his best, clamping his arms around the heaving form until finally, Boogie runs out of sobs and, gasping, recovers his breath. He busies himself behind the counter, fumbling around in the dark and Davy lets him until the dog's head comes up. There's somebody approaching. The Dude knows. Cops, feds or clandestine looters coming back from Merrill's neighborhood? Who?

The intruder tries Weisbuch's front door, turning the knob this way, that way. Coming out from behind the counter, Boogie whimpers. Davy has to shush him. He secured that door as soon as he came in. He puts his hand on the dog's head and the dog understands and settles. Nice dog. Intelligent. He won't bark now, but Boogie is something else.

They can't be here. The Dude will be OK, he can put out food for him, come back for him when this is over, but he and Boogie have to go.

He begins. "It won't be dark much longer." It's like moving a mountain of grief with words. "How about you get up so we can leave?"

Sucked back into his pool of misery, big old Boogie sinks to the floor by the counter and starts sobbing all over again. He truly believes that everybody he cares about got raptured up yesterday except him. They're all up there floating in the sweet hereafter while he is here, grieving for something he doesn't know about.

"Now, OK? Before they get done at the lake." Thinking fast, Davy adds, "There's people running around out there that you don't know, ravaging the neighborhoods, that was probably one of them messing with Marlon's front door just now."

Nothing.

"You don't want them to bust in here and catch us, Boogie, right?"

"Shuh, it don't make no nevermind."

"We don't have much time." He can't leave Boogie alone in here, not the way he is, clinging to the last barstool at the far end of Weisbuch's lunch counter. He's desolate, down enough to jab a fork into his big heart while you weren't looking or hang himself from Weisbuch's ceiling fan.

"If they catch you they'll beat up on you or kick you off the island for good."

"Let me be."

"Don't you get it? They could put you away." The tone he has to use shames Davy but he croons, "You could end up in the state hospital. Do you know what that's like?"

Boogie doesn't care what that's like. "Not going. No way."

Bowing that huge head, he locks his arms around the base of the barstool to make his point.

"Fuck, Boogie. Can you at least stand up and look me in the face?" It's a struggle, but Davy gets him to his feet. "OK then, that's better. Now, let's go."

Snorting up a mess of tears and snot, his big friend hocks up two words. "I can't."

"The hell you can't." Davy plants a hand on his friend's arm, thinking to turn him gently. "OK now, buddy. Move!"

Everything in Boogie explodes all at once. He roars to raise the dead and bring down the living on Weisbuch's store, "I can't!"

"Shit, keep it down, just be quiet, OK? Oh, Boogie, hush!"

Davy's been born, grown old and died several times during this exchange and the more Boogie digs in, the more he knows it's time for them to go out there and look for root causes. Physical evidence. Tracks left by unknown captors. Somebody who saw it happen. Something they left behind.

Boogie tries to shake him off but Davy turns him, aiming him at the front door. "Easy, Boog, OK. OK?" If he can only nudge Boogie to that door, shove him outside . . . "We have to get out of here."

The bubble forming across Boogie's mouth pops and he wails, "I have to stay!"

"For fuck's sake, Boogie, why?" He keeps forgetting that although his handsome friend looks like a grown man he is, at an essential level, somewhere around seven years old.

It's so hard for Boogie and takes him so long to dredge up the right words that Davy could have died and been buried and dug up again by the time he finds the answer. Squeezing it out between sobs, he whispers, "God might come back for me."

"Ooh, Boog." But Davy is grieving too— for everything Boogie should be, that was lost when some fool doctor removed his adenoids and the scalpel cut too deep. More: because at this point he, David Armstrong Ribault, who moved out here from the mainland for the sake of this lovely woman he may never see again— clueless Davy— has no way of knowing exactly how much of his own life is lost along with her.

He makes a frantic grab for Boogie's wrist, digging his nails into the soft tissue so hard that blood comes; he is that desperate to make his point. "Boogie, listen."

"Leave me alone!"

Davy leans in close. He says, "If God loves you he'll find you no matter where you are."

In the next odd second Boogie breaks his grip so fiercely that every joint in his fingers pops. Sobbing, he turns on his old friend Davy, and snarls, baring his teeth like a Rottweiler fixing to rip his face off. He isn't sobbing now. He sets down words meticulously, like a row of cement blocks. "If God loved me, I'd be up there with all the rest of them."

God! Davy yips, "How the fuck do you know?"

"I just know."

Davy digs into his own agnostic heart and heaves the words at Boogie one at a time. "Stubborn *asshole*! You don't. Get this, and let's get out of here. *Nobody knows*."

Boogie bunches his shoulders and rams him in the gut, shoving hard. "I just *know*. And you . . ."

"Wait!"

"And you . . ." He bulldozes Davy out the door and into the street. The last shove is so hard that it almost topples him: "You don't know shit!"

It's true, Davy thinks, waiting for all his breath to knife back into his chest. While he mulls it, Boogie slams the door and shoots the bolt before Davy can, what? Give him the last blessing?

He says anyway, "be safe."

Then he leans against the brick façade, considering. He needs a moment but all he has is whatever time it takes for the first flashlight beams to hit the far end of Bay Street, signifying that they're done at the lake.

It isn't long before voices sift into the muggy pre-dawn air: good old boys, grumbling. He guesses they've dredged, they've sent down divers in scuba gear and failed to stop the volunteers who stripped naked and plunged to the bottom; they've done it all and come up empty. There are no EMT trucks in this procession, so no paramedics working over survivors, nobody carrying stretchers, no gurneys with body bags that he can see. Either everybody he cares about is dead— or worse. Davy studies the matter for a split second too long. Blinded, he ducks as one of the searchers' beams sweeps past. His face gleams like a slab of fresh meat in the light. Someone shouts. Davy runs, but nobody follows. Maybe failure at the lake confused them, he thinks. Or they saw him and don't care.

Unless they're saving him for last.

He can't be here. He can't be on Kraven island, but he can't leave yet. Before he sneaks back to Ray's dock and casts off in the skiff tied up in the shadow of Ray's houseboat, there's one more thing he has to do.

Gone forever or not, bedded down in some new place with Davy's one— and only— love, he realizes. His heart chokes and he has to start over. Gone or hunkered down, conniving to control or destroy Merrill along with Dave Ribault and everybody else, even a man like Rawson Steele doesn't vanish without a trace. Whether he's out there fucking Merrill in the great unknown or masterminding this operation from corporate headquarters; *whether he's holed up right here on Kraven island fixing to bushwhack me, I'll hunt him down and then.* What?

If he has Merrill— wait!

If he's hurt her, I'll kill him dead.

Crazy, but after hours of blundering around the mainland and Poynter's island and the waters off Kraven not knowing, spinning in Merrill's bedroom bereft and ignorant and powerless, he has a place to start.

Nobody inhabits a frilly hotel suite in a small town for more than a week without leaving something behind. Whether Steele engineered this from some big city or got, what— transported with the others— there will be luggage tags in his trash, crumpled papers, bathroom detritus left behind. Before he can quit Kraven island, he has to check out Steele's room at the Harbor City Inn.

He picks up what he needs from the tool drawer at the Caltex station and ducks into the alley that runs along behind storefronts the length of Bay Street, heading for the Inn. They'll be dragging bawling Boogie Hood out of Weisbuch's store by the time Davy comes back this way, gritting his teeth as he skulks along in the shadow of dumpsters, garbage cans, abandoned vehicles, because he's just one guy and he can't stop them and he should have coldcocked Boogie and dragged him out to the boats and left Kraven before they could ever . . .

He should have fought to the death for Boogie and gone down fighting, he should have sprayed them with, OK, what? But they're too many; they're armed and walleyed and belching testosterone and besides, he had *this* to do.

He has to do this and even if he didn't, nothing he does here on the island will stop what's going on, although by God, tomorrow he'll come back with a platoon of Charleston lawyers if he has to, whatever it takes to break Boogie out.

Davy is aware of all this, past and present, as he rushes along. He won't turn on his flash until he's safe, as in, hunched behind the reservations desk at the Harbor City Inn, grateful that Martha Anne Calhoun still records guests' names and room numbers in the ledger her grandfather started the day he got married, to Emily Ann Kidder, and the two of them decorated the renovated Victorian with curly maple and flowered chintz, and opened the hotel. Then he'll break in and search Rawson Steele's second-floor room. That's the easy part. Getting back to Azalea House unseen will be somewhat harder, as he spends too long inside the old hotel, and won't come out until the sun is up, shaken and too conflicted to process the papers he uncovered in Steele's room where, oddly, even his shaving things were still in place.

Working in the dark and working fast, he pulls out certain paperwork he thinks will prove his point, although he's too rattled and exhausted to know exactly what he got. Footsteps hit the hardwood floor below. They're inside. He's out of time. Shaking, he discards the packet of photocopies of Carolina sites and the distressed war-era tintype in a crumbling fake morocco case; they mean nothing to him. He hears voices. Boots on the stairs. Time to hit the back stairs.

He tries to stuff the papers he's found inside his shirt but they're too bulky. He can't run like this. He takes what he can carry and stashes blueprints and site plans in the galvanized Von Harten Dairy box outside the kitchen door. Given the number of early-morning search parties returning from the neighborhoods, he has to back and fill, dive for cover, duck and run all the way to Azalea House, so the mile between here and Ray Powell's dock will take more than an hour to cross.

He can't be sure he hears Boogie's voice above the others as he runs along behind Weisbuch's store; that could be guilt, roaring into his head because it's too late to do anything about it. Wherever he is, Boogie is suffering and even if he wanted to, there's no way he could help.

He's laid wide open now, torn by all the things he's failed to do, he comes thudding onto Ray's property, Azalea House spreads its porches like a Carolina matriarch: whatever you did while I wasn't looking, child, come on in. Davy would like to go in and find Ray, sit down and ask him about the stuff he took, item for item, so Ray can tell him what just happened. Is happening. Will happen, starting now.

He'd like to dump the whole mess on Ray's breakfast table—shuh, he'd like to *eat,* but Ray's long gone and there are cops or looters or both stalking the porches, so he crunches along behind the azaleas with no detours to the water. He wades out in the shadow of the dock.

It's easy enough to untie Ray's skiff. He goes flat against the bottom and lets the current take him out into open water. He won't turn on the auxiliary motor until he thinks it's safe. Then he can head back to Poynter's island, where by this time Earl's up and frying eggs or, if he's lucky and the gods are kind, this morning's catch.

18

Merrill Poulnot
Late

Merrill blinks. *Why do I see myself from a distance?* As if the camera just pulled back.

There's no time for reflection, now that they are in it. Everything is present tense, accent on the *tense*. For the first time since she got here, people fill her sterile living room: Neddy, a study in stop-motion; Steele, vibrating like a hawk arrested in mid-flight; Merrill, poised for whatever comes next.

Ned: "Outside the rim, Mer. For true!"

She gives Steele a long, hard look, as if to see through his pale eyes and into the area behind the saturnine grin, to divine or identify whatever he's hiding, but at this hour in this place, truth is elusive. "Outside the rim," she says. "Really."

"Yep." Steele winks at Ned, as in, Thanks for the setup line. "Pretty much."

Damn that reckless charm. Scowling, she hangs tough. "OK then. Is it the way out of here?"

"One way. Maybe." He spreads his hands. "I'm not sure."

"Then we need to find out."

"OK then." He strips his hoodie and throws it at her head with a *gotcha* grin. "You'll need this."

She snags the thing, but not before it wraps itself around her face like a parasite in a science fiction movie. For a minute, it's hard to breathe. *Not Axe,* she thinks. *God, woman!* It smells of him. "What for?"

He's in the doorway, his face a blur. "While you're waiting." *Waiting for what?*

Weedy Ned's at Steele's elbow with his face taut and his eyes too bright. "Me too, right?"

No. "It's too late. I don't know what's out there."

"Fuck!

You're just a kid! She tries to take his hands in hers, but he pulls away. Tears start. "I have to keep you safe!"

"Fuck!" Her kid brother's head inflates and his fists clench; he's about to self-destruct and when he does, there's no stopping him. She reaches out, trying to make it better, but he shakes her off. "Fuck that, Merrill, bloody fucking fuck!"

Then Steele steps in and sets Ned aside with a simple: "Stay back. You're needed here," and this is strange. The kid backs away, no problem; *he trusts the guy.* Then Steele bends close and mutters into his ear and Ned nods, all business, and backs away. Merrill wonders, but can't ask; her guide is out the door too fast.

He slips out into the dark and she follows. Ned slams the door on her heels as Steele drops off the side of the porch, into the deep shadow of the house.

He takes off, running along in the dark. Won't stop, won't look back.

Like he doesn't care if I come or not. She has no choice. Cold, excited and anxious about leaving Ned in that dismal house, alone and overflowing with unanswered questions, she gulps down fear and plunges after Steele. Bastard, he doesn't even slow down to see whether she made it all right.

It's odd, seeing how he darts in and out between the patches of light, so swift and sure that she wonders when and how he got into the desert soup bowl where they're interned and how, exactly, he knows his way through this surreal landscape, even in the dark. To find out, she has to follow. So she takes out after him, running along in hopes that he'll lead her out of here.

Tearing along like this, blindly following a man she barely knows, Merrill is touchy, uncertain and vulnerable. She's exposed, quivering like a hermit crab turned out of its shell. It's the first time she's come out into the night without Ray Powell walking point. This is weird enough, but there's more. On their forays, Ray always looks out for her. Like a good father, Ray takes the lead, scoping out the route. He won't wave her on until he's gone ahead to make sure it's safe. Not Steele. Whether he's a good man is still in question.

Good or not, the Northerner came to Kraven island with an unspecified link to everything Merrill cares about, and this draws her along. He arrived in the low country with some unstated claim or deep history that so far, he's kept to himself. Standing with Merrill on her front porch on that last night on Kraven island, he was poised to tell her, she thinks. Electric, buzzing with it, teetering on the verge of laying it out, so she'd know. Then Davy pulled up and they were done.

Now he's running so fast that it's hard to keep up. Wait. Is he whistling through his teeth, some old song she almost knows, so she can follow? Who is he? What is this? They've come all the way from the low country to this bleak compound for reasons he can't or won't name, and she doesn't even know what brought him to the border islands, Kraven island in particular. Steele took the lead; it's in his nature, but when Merrill fell in behind him she expected something more, or better from him. Kindness. Explanations, but he won't slow down and he doesn't look back. He rushes on, *tss-tss-tss-tss*-ing as though he could care less whether she follows.

Furious, she puts her head down and lengthens her stride, running so hard that when without warning he stops short she smashes into him, body on body. It's like a little car crash.

She swallows a shout. "Shit!"

He turns on her, swift and urgent. "Shh. We're here."

They are standing in front of a long ersatz-adobe building. It's made on the same plan as the ones lining the plaza, with one difference. There are no outside doors that she can see. No windows and no way in. Hell yes she's mad. "This? You brought me out here to see this? This is nothing!"

"My point."

Everything in her rushes to a dead stop. "And the rim?"

"Oh, that. That's just a story I told the kid," he says, and she has no way of knowing whether this is true. Before she can find the right comeback Steele takes her elbow and steers her behind the utility building, power plant, whatever this place turns out to be that makes it so important. He gestures at a heap of refuse. "In here."

"What?" It looks like nothing to her. Jutting out from the back wall, a row of outsized cartons forms a makeshift annex. It's the first asymmetrical element she's seen in this nowhere place with its relentlessly unbroken planes. Then she understands. Made by human hands. "Your work?"

Stupid, expecting him to answer. Pulling a Maglite out of nowhere, he opens a flap in the biggest of the boxes and waves her inside. "Quiet. It's something you need to know about."

"I don't see anything."

"Please. This is where we wait."

She considers her options: turn back. Go into this corrugated shipping crate and deal with whatever comes of it. Merrill has made it through her life in one piece so far because anxiety and remembered grief make her resourceful. She deals in fallback plans, and she's quick to devise them. In split seconds her mind scurries here, there, and comes back with one. Given the man, the hour, her options, she ducks into the unknown, thinking, *Lady, it's a* carton. If she has to, she can topple the thing and crawl out the bottom or punch her way out, banging at the corners until the tape gives— or, oh shit, what if this thing is stapled together? Then she'll . . .

As it turns out, she won't have to do any of these things. Steele stands aside as she enters and waits for her to settle before he follows. The thing is bigger than a piano crate, big enough to hold a forklift, but she has no time to speculate about how it got here or what it used to contain.

Inside, he waves her to a Styrofoam cooler positioned by the exit and hunkers down on the far side of the carton, setting a safe distance between them, as in: *whatever you're thinking, I won't*. Then he sets the Maglite on the ground between them with the beam aimed at the cardboard overhead, creating enough light for her to see him clearly. Like a magician, he makes a quick gesture: *nothing up my sleeves,* showing empty palms. At least he spares her the slick, performer's smile.

Nothing about this is feasible; the constricted space, the fact that it's below freezing in here and even colder outside; that she can see her breath but Steele is easy with it, sitting there in a sweatshirt, grinning as though the cold desert night can't touch him.

Measuring credulity, Merrill says, "You live here?"

"No. This is where I watch."

What!

She can't speak. There are more questions than there are words: when and how he arrived in this— there is no right word for this place; she needs to know why he wasn't dumped in the same spot at the same time as every other soul on Kraven island the day they arrived; whether in fact, he was an advance man for whatever seized them or just another victim, caught in the wrong place. Waiting in his oversized carton with nothing between them but the harsh beam of the Maglite, Merrill strangles on the central question, the one that surfaces no matter how hard she tries to choke it down. There are too many possibilities, and this one terrifies her.

What if he caused all this?

Who are you, really? One of us, or something else?

The next thing he says to her answers no questions, but it blows her doubts to hell.

"I packed the tintype to show you, but when this thing happened, it got, um. Left Behind. Never mind, they had the photographer make two. If you don't have it your dad does, that's for true." So odd: he sounds like somebody from home. "My great-great-whatever and his best friend Hampy home from the Citadel, two Charlton kids all brave and don't-mess-with-me in their dress blues and slouch hats with the ostrich plumes, fixing to go to war. Pictures of their new husbands to give the girls they left behind."

She stuffs her knuckles into her mouth.

"You *have* seen it, right?"

The hell of it is, she has! Her great-grandmother Poulnot kept the image in its velvet pouch stored in the ancestral brass-bound box that Grandmother passed down; it came through the generations until the last Hampton Poulnot . . . Merrill winces.

He doesn't exactly smile. "Southerners do love to pass these things down."

Exact phrase. She thinks: *That doesn't mean* . . . But it does.

"Two best friends in their new uniforms, all cleaned up for the man with the magic box. You know. In case they didn't come home." Is it her imagination or is he grinning that same jaunty grin she saw on the young rebel officer's face?

"They made it back the first time, at least. Else we wouldn't be here."

Yes she knows what he is claiming; she thinks, *I would. Would you?*

"It came down in my family through the generations, but there were complications, and I only just got mine."

"What?"

"Yours is still around, for true."

Raging at her the night she moved out for good, Father ripped the case in two pieces and threw it into the fire, but it's not like she'll explain.

"Hey," he says, grinning, "I owe you one. If the first Hampton Poulnot hadn't dragged my great-great-great-great off the field when he did, I wouldn't be here. Mine was named . . ."

She completes it from memory, "Archie Rivard. It's on the note . . ."

And he finishes, ". . . in the back of the tintype case. It's short for Archbold."

"I know."

The air between them changes, but it's nothing they said. At the first subtle vibration, his head comes up.

She begins, "You're his . . ." when he lunges.

"Shhh!"

Everything in her shudders to a stop. Even after he retreats to his corner she can feel the warmth of the hand he just clapped across her mouth— not gentle, exactly, but sure. Silenced, she listens as the building at his back comes to life. What comes next is too subtle to be heard, but the vibration penetrates her to the bone. It's as though the installation, the air surrounding and the sky above it are located somewhere deep in the guts of an infinite, mysteriously soundless MRI, and the great machine is imaging— what?

It is in this cold, intensely physical period of stasis, confined in a tight space with Rawson Steele, who is a stranger to her in spite of shared history, that she senses Davy— nothing they said— just a physical memory of the two of them, body on body, Merrill and her lover back when they were at their best, indestructible, locked together as though nothing could change or even threaten what they thought they had.

In spite of the context or perhaps because of it— Rawson Steele, *this close*— sense memory warms her in the inevitable way, and this is both sweet and tremendously sad. Without being aware of it, she slips into the zone. Sitting with her head bent and her hands clamped between her knees, she hears, frames and re-frames and rehearses certain soft words she will say to make things right, when she and Davy . . . If.

He says what you say. "Are you OK?"

"What?" She snaps back into herself, blinking.

It's too dim in here for him to see her clearly, but his tone changes. "Was it good for you?"

Is he laughing at me? Anger drives her to her feet.

"Sit down. You can't go out right now."

"The hell I can't."

"We can't." Standing, he fills the carton. "This happens every night. We have to lay low until it's over. The sweep. Now, shut up and sit down."

"Why?" They face off in a collision of wills, Merrill with her fists bunched to fight, or wring some truth from him. It's like confronting a large, intelligent dog; you don't know whether he's trying to protect you or what. Exasperated, she backs into the Styrofoam cooler and sits. Steele moves back into place and drops to his haunches as though equalizing their positions, but he's not about to answer. In the end, Merrill breaks the long silence, "OK. What sweep?"

"Believe me, you don't want to be out there. Let me put it another way. If you get picked up, I can't help you."

This raises more questions, but she's too rattled to ask him who or what sweeps the installation or what foreign bodies it sweeps away or why a sweeper is needed at all in this relentlessly pristine trap. Brooding, she rehearses questions while Steele sits patiently, listening for something Merrill won't recognize and may not be able to hear.

Then she does. The whirr is just loud enough to tell her that something huge is passing. She catches a glint of light reflected in its metal flank— just a flash, seen through a crack created by the monstrous instrument or machine as it nudges Steele's makeshift shelter, veers around the foreign object and glides on. Merrill's mind does that thing it does when things get too intense: she flashes on an image she knows— the Roomba she bought Father, as though a blind vacuum cleaner could make a dent in the dirt accumulating in the house she fled.

As the sound recedes she collects herself; she has to leave! Before she can start up, Steele brings her down with one hand, not the way Father would, not like Davy. "No." He lets go at once, but the warmth of his hand imprints her. "Not until they've swept the perimeter. Stay. They're almost done."

How do you know?

They face off in silence. Finally, he says offhand: "We can't go yet, but it's OK to talk."

By this time there are so many issues boiling up, pressing questions backed up and waiting, that they fill her throat and she can't speak. When she manages to cough one up, of all the answers she can't get and needs to know, what comes to the top isn't what she intended. It's not what she wants at all.

She needs to stop, rethink, but at these close quarters and in this dim light, this bothers her the most. It comes out with such force that as it explodes between them, she notes Steele's immediate, reflexive flinch:

"What were you digging for?"

19

Ned

Dawn

Fuck, shit. Crap, shitass son of a bastard bitch, fucking fuck-face and every other pissed-off combo I'm too messed up to get back right now, this totally blows. I was up all night but there's a whole chunk of it that I can't remember. What's up with that? Do they gas us nights, or pipe in worse things that we don't know about, or did I just slag off and accidentally take a nap and they came back and left all over again while I was knocked out?

Whatever, Merrill, wherever you are. Whatevs.

I'm awake now, shit, it's almost light out and the only person here is me. Where the fuck are they? Rawson told me, sit tight and he'd come back and get me, but it's been forever and there's no sign. My big sister just up and took off with my new best friend, the only one I have in this rotten hole, if he really is my friend, which, I am beginning to wonder.

If we were real friends he'd be back by now.

And there's nothing to eat! Merrill's crap white fridge in her dead white kitchen is dead empty, I looked. No leftovers, not even noshies like you serve with drinks, plus there's nothing in the dumbwaiter, what's up with that? Does their searchbot scope all our houses at night and they just know, or did she leave out a note, like, DON'T BOTHER? What was she thinking? I could starve to death and she wouldn't give a crap.

If Merrill cared she would be back by now just like she promised. Yeah, right.

Like Merrill ever keeps her promises, like the ones she made the night she left home for good, with me still in it. OK, she did promise that Patrice would live in and keep care of me, Mer paid time and a half out of her college fund to make it happen, but it didn't last. After a while, Patrice couldn't hack it. Too much Father and she was done, but until last week she came out and did for us every day; we both felt bad and promised to stay in touch, but, you know. So Merrill promised to keep an eye on me and him, she said if Father got bad, all I had to do was call her. As if! She was never home. OK, after that one time she said, If you can't reach me and you won't call the cops, go straight to the ER, the X-ray will help us in court. Or get the whole thing on the answering machine: evidence! All we have to do is play it back for the cops and Judge Brock. They'll give me custody for sure, and that's a promise.

All I had to do was pick up that phone. Like I would do that. He's my fucking father, yo.

I begged her to stay back at the house along with me but she said, I can't be that person and when I said, What person, she just teared up and said, "It's hard to explain." If he was messing with her she wouldn't tell, at the time I was too little and stupid to know.

Shit hey, I could of showed her how to bring down a man twice her size, I learned that in the Koro Ishi, we trained for worse things back in the dojo. I could of showed her, but, shit, I was never sure that what I think is what she really meant. Listen, Merrill ran out on me back then, so what if she was crying when she did it, I'm not showing her shit. Then her and that

Rawson took off from here like shit sliding down a shingle last night, and if you think I'm over it, well, fuck you.

If there was anything in this place sharper than a spork, I would slash all her shit to ribbons, starting with the white fluffyruffle curtains and the flibberty quilt on the flat, empty bed in her dead white bedroom.

Fuck that shit, I'm not staying here just because they said. My man Rawson came on to me all man to man, like, "We're in this together," and I was so stupid that I thought he actually gave a crap.

If he gave a crap, they'd be back by now.

Unless.

Get out! *Unless!* No way. I'm not going there.

It's cold and lonely and hungry as hell in here, plus, in another minute that sun will pop up outside like a great flaming ostrich egg and if I try to go home, I'll be fried like pork sausage before I can make it, which . . .

Why would I go back there?

That isn't home. It's just another place with Father in it. Our first night, when her and Ray Powell shut me and Father in together and walked away, I thought, At least this one is clean. I thought that *clean* meant it would be better, but except for the extreme silence, which was a ginormous load off after all the ranting, oh right, and the no whiskey, Father is pretty much the same. He quit talking and he doesn't hit anymore. He doesn't even get mad, but it's all backed up inside that big white head of his, and I think he's fixing to blow.

The minute they shut the door on us he went all still and glassy-eyed. He's spent all day and half the night in that tombstone chair ever since, staring into the shiny white tabletop and puking up words nonstop, but so low that I can't exactly make them out. He probably *looks* reformed or whatever from being in there with nothing to drink but milk or water and nobody but me to push around, but he could just as easily rear back and rip my ears off. All the old poison's still in there. It, like, *compressed* in his belly and his chest and it's filling him up 'til there's noplace left for it to go but OUT. Fuck yes I am scared of him.

I can't stay here, but no way am I going back there.

Wait.

There's Ray. Thank God there's always Ray.

I'll go to Ray's. Me and Rawson that *I thought was my friend* followed him home the night my smartass new best friend dropped his phone and we cut and ran. Ray came around the corner and scooped it up just as we went around the other end, so we laid back and followed him home. We were almost there when Rawson mumbled words I didn't get and we had to turn back, but I think I can find the place.

Rawson, you never know, but you can always count on Ray Powell. Him and me, we'll find Merrill and when we do, boy, she'd better have a fucking good excuse. OK, at least he'll have food. Plus, guys like Ray always get their phone or computer first because they're so important; he'll have one, if who or whatever's doing this to us is handing them out.

It takes way too long to find Ray's place, these fucking white boxes all look alike. It's scary outside and cold as fuck, which it always is until the sun starts up and like to roasts you on a spit. I have to hurry! I go running along, running along, searching for the one thing that makes Ray's house different, *he leaves his shutters open, like: nothing to be afraid of, nothing to hide,* so I'll know it when I . . .

Holy fuck!

One of those front doors bangs wide— *Ray's door!* It's like a smack to the head. Then a long and terrible noise blows out of the house in a mess of words. Words come rolling down the steps like rocks in an avalanche, and it stops me cold. It's Father, bawling like Jonah, right after the whale yacked him up. My fucking father shoots out of Ray's front door, whiter than death and shivering in his dead white scrubs which . . . Which!

There's a great big monstrous *splotch* on the front of his scrubs. Fuck, is that blood?

When he sees me he lunges down the steps and smashes into me, going, "Don't go in there," as he shoves me back and back, all the way back down that walk leading away from the house. "Don't go in there, in the name of God!"

Fuck! "What is it, Father, *stop that!* Father, what?"

He won't stop shoving and he won't say. "Bad, Edward. It's bad."

"What's wrong, what's wrong?" I need to see, I'm scared to see, I don't want to know, I'm slobbering-crazy because there's something terrible in there and I don't know what. "Ray? What is it? Where's Ray?"

He plants his big, flat hand in my chest like a STOP sign. "You don't want to know!"

My heart shrivels up. "Did you hurt him?"

Dead eyes, the father looks at me with round, dead eyes. "No."

But he knows something I don't know, and I want to kill him dead. I'm not asking, I'm telling. *"What did you do to him."*

"No." He keeps pushing me back, back out into the street, and for the first time ever he isn't shitty or pissed off at me, he's something worse, that I don't know the name of. "Just. No."

I run at the old bastard yelling "Shut up," because I don't want to hear, I'm flat-out begging because I don't want to know, "Shut up, shut up, I need to know!"

"No," he says, and after all that, Father is so quiet that it scares the crap out of me. "You don't."

And I can't help it, I go, "You fucking motherfucking son of a fucking fartface fucking fuck . . ." It just comes pouring out; I hate him so hard that I run out of words because I don't know how it happened and I don't know who did it, but my friend Ray's still in there, and he can't help anybody now.

I choke on clots of muck, I cough them up and I stumble. Father grabs me by the hoodie and yanks me back on my feet. I'm like to strangle and too fucked up to fight. At least I don't cry.

Then OMG Father, the great white Moses of Kraven island, Father turns into the great white Avenger. He shoves me with one fist jammed in the back of my neck, so I stumble down the street while he steams along until finally he whips me around and drags me instead. Then he goes running up front walks, yanking me up the steps while he pounds on doors to wake up the living, roaring to raise the dead. "Out, God damn you. Emergency!"

"Let go. You're scaring me!"

No way. Everything my father is, everything he kept backed up inside him from the day his so-called *people* turned against him until today, rolls up in his throat and explodes into the street and I get that he'll do anything to get them back.

"Out," he screams. "Out, in the name of Ray Powell, come out!"

After weeks of silence my father is larger than life and bellowing like eight hundred trumpets, all Noah and Moses and every one of the Avengers on a stick, with me bumping along behind him like a stuffed toy, all hurt and no bones. Everything he had backed up inside him crashes and pours out in a massive, supercharged rant. It won't matter how hard I kick at his ankles or try to wrestle out of the iron claw, he is monumental, and I can't stop him. It's awful and kind of like, *regal*. Like there are minions with drums and trumpets ahead of him, clearing the way.

First nothing happens, but as we cross the next street, something does. Doors in front of us open to Father, and behind us, people straggle out into the fresh air in ones and twos, rubbing their eyes and blinking like something that just hatched. The next thing I know, they're falling in behind my fucking father, who has turned into a walking war-trumpet.

When the crowd forms up for real and Father's sure they're following he lets go of me and blasts off, hellbent for it.

Control.

Outside like this, on the loose for the very first time, he is his own loudspeaker, running along bellowing, "MURDER, YOU IDIOTS. MURDER MOST FOUL!" It's weird and terrifying, watching them fall in with the others, gathering mass and thumping along with only the sound of their breath huffing and the thud of their feet. After all these weeks indoors, they would have followed him anywhere, which makes him yell louder as he goes:

"SOMEBODY MURDERED RAY POWELL."

All their voices come back all at once: "Murder!"

Then he goes, "AND I KNOW WHO."

And his fucking people are all, buddabuddabudda, thoughts feeding words so fast that all my back hairs rise up as it comes out in a chant, "He knows, he knows, he knows," marking the beat to my father's rant, as— like that!— ordinary citizens of Kraven island follow the Power.

Father's legs pump up and down like cranks on the wheels of a steam engine, chuff, chuff, chuff. Then, my God, my God, more neighbors, assholes who haven't been out of their square white boxes since Day One come out and fall in behind him, tens and dozens of people I haven't seen in weeks piling out into the fresh air with their legs going up and down, up and down like Father's, marching along in their white scrubs.

Then Father screams:

"I SAW HIM."

And I think, *Oh, shit!*

They all go, "saw him, he saw him, he saw him . . ." Another couple of blocks like this and he'll have every one of them mashed up tight behind him chanting "theymurdered theymurdered," and "hesawhim . . . sawhim sawhim . . ." which makes me feel extremely weird, as in, scared and excited all at once. Then he yells, "THERE'S A KILLER OUT HERE," and holy fuck, everybody else starts yelling too, "*there's-a-killer-theresakillertheresakiller*" making that scary engine sound that warns you, *Here I come, get out of the way,* and where ten minutes ago they hated him for what he did in the plaza, Father has gone all Moses and turned the whole mess of humanity into an engine of destruction, roaring along like a runaway train.

They run through the streets thudding along all rhythmic and terrible, and the noise that comes out of them, WUH, WUH, WUH— sounds like *killkill kill,* although nobody's actually said it yet; then we pull up short in the plaza and oh, shit! Father screams. "We have to get him!" and people *I used to know* turn into a murderous machine, blaring, "Get him," louder and louder, over and over, "Gethimgethimgethim. Get him, get him!" until Father jumps up on the base of the flagpole and raises his hand like a fucking prophet and, son of a bitch, they all shut up all at once.

"Yes!" Father shouts, like some kind of Holy Roller, "It's the Northerner!"

And his people shout, "It's the Northerner!"

He's so far into it that I get sucked in and dragged along, "First he tried to steal our island!"

"Robberrobberrobber."

God, does it all pile up in them then, all the shit that's come down since we ended up here, the heat, the cold, the stupid food and the fucking scrubs and whatever kept us all inside our stupid houses, even I was getting mad, we're all yelling, "First he stole our island . . ."

Father brings down his arm like a baton. "And now this!"

So everybody is all, "And now this," because they're here instead of home and we are fucking sick of it. They are Father's people now.

Somehow Father's made it up on big old Delroy Root's wide shoulders again, but this time nobody is about to drag him down because Father is in charge and he is screaming, "THERE IS EVIL IN THIS PLACE."

"Evil in this place!" They are in it now, "evil in this place," repeating, repeating, "evil in this place" while I go silent because there really is evil in this place, but it's not what they think.

Then the old man hoists himself higher so he is almost standing, rising to a screaming climax that splits me wide and strikes me in the heart because this is Father, and he did see us sneaking out last night, me and my new best friend. "There is evil in this place and evil did this. Evil killed Ray Powell and evil put us here. Last night I looked evil in the face and its name is . . ."

In the intense pause that follows, I hear the sound of a hundred people holding their breath.

Then Father splits the skies with it: "Its name is Rawson Steele," and, God

Rawson Steele, right now, even I believe.

"Rawson Steele, Rawson Steele, Rawsonsteele . . ." The

mutter runs through them like a tidal wave but there's a careful fufufuh because, not counting Father last night, when me and Rawson walked right past him and out that front door and he watched without blinking, only Merrill knew that Rawson Steele is here with us in east buttfuck, and that doesn't mean that the guy I thought was my friend actually killed Ray Powell, like, *murdered* the only real friend I ever had in my life and I didn't know it— at least I think it doesn't, but there's no stopping Father now.

Wrong or not, the mean old bastard raises that arm again and brings it down like the flag at a NASCAR speedathon, bellowing, "Are you with me?"

And everybody except me is going huff-Huff-HUFF; they're, like, *inflating,* getting big and loud enough to fill the space and overflow the desert beyond it with their huge and terrible: "YES!"

20

"Man." Easy in bleached denim, easy in his life, Earl Pinckney stands on his front porch, watching his old friend wade in from the swash. Davy comes up the bank in one of Ray Powell's golfing outfits, wet to the knees of Ray's marine green cotton pants. "You look like shit."

Grinning, he gives Earl the finger but a blind fool would see that Davy has the shakes, and not because the water's cold. It's like bathwater out there in the swash.

Earl gives him a minute before he asks, "What was it like?"

"Empty. It was like the island died."

"You mean, *they* died?"

"I don't think so. Just— everything that they . . ." He can't finish.

"Say what?"

"That they left behind." He struggles to find the right words, but facts keep sliding around. "Like the soul of the island just— went out."

" 'Od damn, Ribault." Typical Earl, trying to keep the tone light. "So, what? Did we miss the rapture or was it space aliens?"

"Don't."

"You're not going to explain, are you?"

166 • KIT REED

"I can't!" *Deaf, dumb and blind boy,* David Ribault. Can't think, can't speak . . .

"Dude!"

Urgency rushes in to fill the empty space. A thought jump-starts, "I've got to . . ." and the sentence dies. It's a fucking imperative, and Dave Ribault is standing here going mwah mwah mwah like a koi fish because he can't choke out the words he needs to finish this one. He knows it's: **got to do something major,** but exhaustion sneaked up and murdered his brain while he was out there drifting around in Ray's skiff and he doesn't know what it is.

Whatever the *it* is, it's important. No, essential.

Knows: **Got to do that**— but he has no idea what.

"You OK?"

Or where to start, Dave Ribault, shaking his head like a wet coon hound. Arf. "I'm fine!"

Earl gives him a long, hard look. Like a good nurse, his best friend says, "Let's get you inside."

"Your mom won't mind?"

"Not much she does mind, being how she is."

"Shit."

"Pretty much."

As they pass through the front room, Theda Pinckney looks up from the sofa, beaming. "Hello boys. How was school?"

"Same as it ever was, Mom." Earl gives her a big smile and hurries Davy past. To Davy, she looks the same. "It was fine."

"Do you have homework?"

"Not today, Mom. I did it in study hall."

"Man, I'm sorry."

"She's happy, wherever she is." Earl waits until he has Davy settled at the kitchen table. Slips a juice box in front of him.

Waits for him to drink it and then waits a little longer for the sugar to kick in. He says, "Dude, they took your car."

"Say *what*?"

"They damn-all cleared the island of everything that rolls and everybody that's not from here. Won't matter who you are or what you tell them. If you don't have that great big **Resident** plate on your bumper, you're screwed."

The sun goes on shining in on Earl's kitchen table, same as it ever was. In the next room Theda Pinckney sits in front of her TV, rapt, although the screen is dark. "Fuck."

"They towed yours away last night and when they check the exit list and you're not on it, they'll come looking for you."

"The cops?"

"Any yoohoo with a gun and a badge, given the way things are. They can't get to Kraven island and they can't go home, so they're all over Poyntertown like white on rice. Packing, every damn one of them, scared shit and loaded for bear. It's lame, but if they catch you, you're screwed."

Right. Getting here took longer than he thought. Hours wasted in that skiff, drifting until it was safe to sit up and row, and it was never safe, going flat every time police boats chewed up the waves or he heard the vibrations of another plane; hours of idle frustration and the weight of lost time turn Dave into a blunt instrument. He stands with his jaw set and his fists tight. "Because?"

But you don't do Earl like that. He puts on his easy, *Don't ask me, I just work here* face, going all Gullah on him all over again, translation, *don't fuck with me.* "Dude, they got so many theories they ain-fuh takin chances. We in Red Alert."

Running ahead of the unknown, short on sleep and sick with confusion, Davy lets it all out. "Don't do me like that, mofo. Just don't!"

Earl takes a good long look at him. "Shit, Dave. I'm sorry. You're worse off than I thought."

"I'm OK."

"Have it your way. Now sit the fuck down and I'll make you a BLT." Earl glares until Davy backs into a chair. He slides a coffee in front of the refugee, fugitive, whatever this week has made of him and spends too long on the sandwich, making time for Davy to reconsider and regroup. He works silently, laying out crisp bacon on paper towel to absorb the grease; he toasts whole grain bread, washes the lettuce and slices his tomato while the bacon drains and assembles the sandwich with just enough butter and mayo to make it hang together. He cuts it neatly and sets it down in front of his friend.

Davy's gone off somewhere inside his head, so Earl just starts. "I'm not shitting you about the theories. We got experts coming out our ears. Feds and psychics and shrinks are on it, PhDs in every known science in the mortal universe are studying this thing. They can't stop sounding off and every goddam one of them has a different idea, fools theorizing 24/7, and they don't know shit. They're talking everything from mass hallucination to the Rapture— oh wait, same thing. Third-world conspiracy, Them ganging up on Us. Bad doings in some government lab. Plague, your people running off somewhere they won't get it. Nobody out here knows what came down or whether the government is behind it or God or the Russians or fucking Martians, it's crazy out there."

Pre-occupied, drowsing in the familiar, comfortable kitchen, Davy hears what the dog hears: *blarg blarg blarg.*

Like a worried kid, Earl spreads his hand: *How many fingers?* "You in there?"

"Back off, I'm cool."

"It's crazy out there and we don't know shit. We can't rightly find out, either. TV's out, phone towers are stone dead, something killed 'em and we can't get a fucking signal, damn radio's useless now. Signal jammers from here to east Jesus. It's a security thing."

This brings Davy back. "How do you get your news?"

"Any way we can." Earl nudges the sandwich plate. "Eat, goddammit."

Dutifully, he picks up the BLT.

"Governor thinks it's third-world pirates, like in Somalia; he's got 'em all up there in Columbia, state of emergency, you'd think it was World War Twelve. They're sitting around in the state house waiting for the ransom note."

"Like you could kidnap a hundred people all at once." Davy's hands are sliding around with the sandwich, shaky, like snakes he can't control. No surprise. He puts it down. "What do you think happened?"

"Could be this could be that, nobody thinks the same thing; some people think they just ran into the water at the end of the point. State thinks pirates, D.C. thinks otherwise, government agencies are looking at it eight ways to Sunday but it's not like they're going to come out and tell you anything. State Health and Human Services thinks they all cleared out ahead of the plague, but like, how?"

"What if they really did walk into the sea?"

"Don't be an asshole. Could be they're locked up in a lab somewhere, like it really is science. It's not like they took off in anything with a black box or sonar or transmissions that you can trace, and their phones? Forget it. No trace of a GPS. They're just missing is what they are, like those people in that plane. They spent close to a billion hunting those poor souls."

"Which plane?"

"The one that they never found. Those people are still out there, for all anybody knows."

Davy's belly sinks. "They're all dead."

"How they're gonna prove that? When people go missing, you never know. It's not like they got stolen, they didn't run away. They're not dead. Until proved otherwise, they're just gone."

Davy rages. "There's gotta be a reason."

"They're still out there, get it!" Earl spreads his hands on the table. *Nothing to see here, nothing up my sleeves.* "They're just not anywhere."

Still out there. Davy comes back into himself. "Boogie saw something."

"The flash?"

"Something like it. In the sky."

"Dude, everybody thinks they saw something. Theda says it was blue."

"Wait!"

Earl sighs. "But you know how Theda is."

Davy does. It's sad. "Yeah, but Boogie . . ."

"People think they saw something, they didn't unelse they did. Meanwhile the DOD called a code red, so we're pretty much locked down. Kraven is quarantined and we're some kind of embargoed, nobody gets on Poynter's from either bridge, they're patrolling the channel, copters above and boats below . . ."

Davy cuts him off. "I know."

". . . and everybody that doesn't belong here has to go. I love you, man, but it's not safe. Dude, you've never seen paranoia like this. Lauren says . . ."

Davy doesn't get depressed, but the shadow of the black raptor blows across his face.

Earl breaks off. "Shit, I'm sorry."

It's my fault she's gone. "It's no big."

"I took half your sandwich."

"No prob." Rocked by loss, Dave Ribault sits in front of his untouched half, considering. It's quiet and comfortable here in Earl Pinckney's house, with light striking the golden oak table where they sit. The first Gaillard Pinckney finished it by firelight the year he built the place and the third or fourth sanded and shellacked it and brought it to a shine. If he runs his hand along the bevel, he can trace the skulls he and Earl gouged into the wood when they were twelve, crude proofs of the existence of Earl Pinckney and Dave Ribault running up the heels of initials carved into the wood by generations of Pinckneys that came before, like proofs of the existence of God.

Earl stays on Poynter because of his mother; they both know he could make better music in Nashville or New Orleans and hit the top of the charts: recordings, videos, world concert tour, he's that good, but Earl's OK. If he lived anywhere that he couldn't look out on open water, he'd dry up and drift away. His aunt Maida comes in nights to stay with Theda so he can be with Lauren at her house; he loves his work and he loves to fish, he loves Lauren Pottinger enough to say so without hesitation or misgivings; they're getting married next fall and after the wedding Theda will move in with her sister Maida, who's been lonely since Jake died, everything neatly settled while idiot Davy, no, fuck the kid nickname, he's thirty-two. Idiot Dave Ribault, assaholic indecisive full-grown shit, while Earl . . .

It all piles in on him, but that's not what comes out. "Boogie's still out there. They hunted him down and caught him like a dog." He chokes on the rest. "They grabbed him and I didn't do shit to stop it. I let it come down."

"Poor kid."

"He's forty-five."

"You know what I mean."

"That's not the worst of it," Dave says, but does not explain. Good thing he doesn't have to. He can't.

"What do you want me to do?"

"Just let me hang in here until night. I'm going back."

"Why the fuck?"

"I have to."

Earl doesn't ask him how. "Not yet. They're still out there, tracking stragglers. You could end up like Boogie, or worse."

"OK then. Tonight."

"Earl Calhoun Pinckney, what have you two been up to?"

Earl looks up, astounded. "Mom!"

Theda Pinckney glides in for a landing behind her son's chair. "You look like something the cat dragged in."

"We didn't either of us hear you," Earl says.

She is groping her way back from a past that neither of them knew or could imagine and— thank God— stalled in a past they remember. "Your little friend looks even worse than you do. Honey, does your mom know you're over at Earl's?"

"It's Dave, Miz Pinckney. Dave Ribault."

"Of course you are!" She gives him a lovely, crumpled smile. "I'll make you some of my poached eggs, and you'll feel better."

"That's real sweet of you, Ma'am, but I just ate."

"Don't worry, Mom. I'm keeping care of him."

Theda's aged to the point of transparency; for the first time Dave looks at her and thinks: *frail*. The soft velour suit hangs loose now, but the color matches her eyes and her smile's the same, a little uncertain but sweet, sweet. She clamps both hands on the back of Earl's chair to steady herself and goes on as though they're still twelve and she's herself again. "Oh, you boys. You just *laugh* and have the best time!"

"Nice to see you, Ma'am."

The spark ignites. For a flash-second, Theda Pinckney is who she used to be. "Don't say 'Ma'am.' You make me feel old!" Then she tightens her grip on the back of Earl's chair, and as Dave watches, whatever carried her this close to real life floats right out of her and she slumps, clinging to the chair.

Davy's hands fly out. *Oh, Ma'am. Ma'am!*

Earl gets up carefully, steadying his chair so his mother won't shift off-balance and topple. He takes her by the elbow so firmly that Dave flinches.

Reflexively, she clamps his hand to her side.

Earl has been here so many times before that what comes next is a smooth, practiced operation. Gentle loosening of the arm, to free his hand. Careful maneuver to turn her and get her moving. Dave gets up to help and with a gracious smile she offers him her other elbow; together, they nudge her along an inch at a time, and like a dancer, she yields.

"It's OK, Mom. OK. Let's get you back to your chair."

Which would have been it, but both men are so focused on the delicate transaction that the slam of a car door outside is lost in the blast of the TV set coming back to life.

Theda hears. She lifts her head. "Who is it? Who's there?"

"Nobody, Mom."

"Who's out there?"

"Nobody. It's fine."

No to both.

A scruffy supernumerary peers through the screen door as he pounds on the wood. With afternoon sunlight bouncing off the water at his back, he looks like the Pillsbury Doughboy in silhouette, fixing to pop out when the can explodes. "Police."

"Shit."

"Language, Earl. Company!"

"Hide," Earl says without moving his face, and Dave dodges into the kitchen.

"Son, it's *company*."

"I know you're in there."

"Hang on."

"It's company, honey." Theda paddles air, blinking. "Aren't you going to make your manners and let him in?"

With Dave out of sight, Earl pushes his mother backward into her spot on the sofa, filling the empty moment with: "Who are you, and what do you want?"

"Don't fuck with me, I'm the fucking police."

"I said, hang on, I have a sick woman here!" He takes his sweet time patting her in place. He waits for her to settle. Then he goes.

"That car you hid in the woods ain't there. It's in impound down to the harbor . . ." the rent-a-cop says with a loaded look over Earl's shoulder, scoping the living room: *I know you're in there*. "In case the owner wants to know."

"Who?"

"The owner." Fool rattles paper at him. Registration? Could be. "One Donald Reeboat."

"Nobody I know. Now stand down."

"Is he here?"

"What did I just tell you?"

"I know he's in there."

"I said, stand down!"

"I know you're in there, come out or I'll shoot."

Backed into the wedge between the refrigerator and the wall, Dave can't see the door but he knows Earl is facing off with the rent-a-cop, pissed off and stretched too thin. In another minute one man will lunge through the screen and attack the other, and it could just as easily be Earl. Dave's heard it before and he knows the tune. He tenses, set to throw himself into it, separate them, coldcock the cop or throttle him to get this over with, whatever it takes.

But Theda Pinckney knows the tune better than Dave. She wails, "Oh." Then she rises up and staggers out to meet the enemy, shrieking, "Oh, oooh, oh! Somebody help me please, I'm dying, I'm choking, get the doctor, somebody, get 911!" All panicky old lady starved for breath and choking like to die, Theda howls to the heavens and crumples, and even Dave could not tell you whether her emergency is real.

"Oh, lady." The angry lump in the doorway is freaking. His voice shatters and falls to bits. "We can't get 911. We can't get nothing by phone."

Earl pounces. "Then get out of here and don't come back until you get help. Find a doctor! Unless you want to do the mouth-to-mouth yourself."

"I can't get no . . ."

"If Momma dies, it's on you!"

Dave hears trouble running for the car.

No need to help Theda. She sits up, grinning.

"Mom?"

Dave comes at them with his arms wide. "Ma'am, Ma'am!" Love hits him dead center. *You were magnificent.*

It takes them a while to get her to her feet and back to the sofa. In the fragile seconds before she lapses into what she was when he first came in, Theda says, "You boys had better scoot before he comes back."

21

Merrill
Later

This is just wrong. They are sitting too close in a wooden shed, Merrill and the Northerner who . . . This is a sentence she can't finish. The slatted walls, the clutter are at odds with the purity of the tidy desert enclave where she's lived ever since . . . How long has it been? In time either compressed or expanded by anxiety, Merrill has lost track. She's wedged in chockablock with Rawson Steele, in . . .

In terms of exact location, she's lost. Even the packing crate where he first led her had a certain logic to it, but this is new. They're sitting so close that she can feel the warmth. Still as he is in this new place, the man is whistling somewhere behind his teeth; she knows the tune. Once she's grounded— grounded?— the words will come back, problem being that she has no idea where she is or what this is.

It's nothing like the uniform cubes in the compound. The houses that contain and control their lives sit shoulder to shoulder like good soldiers or ice cubes, tightly sealed against sun and sand and the unforeseeable, flying debris and disruptive elements— strangers, new ideas— that blow in on the desert wind. This is nothing like his packing-carton lair. There's sand seeping into this new place: sand in her hair and sand on the dank prison floor.

If, in fact, they are trapped here.

She doesn't know, any more than she knows how she got here. Minutes ago she was hunkered down with Steele in his cardboard shack. Now she isn't. Did she black out? What? Now, they could be anywhere. Lit by LED strips bolted to four-by-fours overhead, the shed is at odds with everything in the compound where they landed, if landing is what they did.

Beggared for words, she corrects. *Arrived.*

In all their forays, she and Ray Powell never saw anything like this. In the last few days the two of them covered most of the territory inside the rim, troubled by the relentlessly clean lines, the sterile sameness, trying to figure out how they fit into the design. Groggy as she is, she thinks: *If only you were Ray.* Her tough, steady, impeccable friend would help her sort this out. No. He'd help her sit the fuck up. Why is she so weak? She's slumped on the floor with no idea how she got here or how long it's been, propped against Rawson Steele like a rag doll discarded by a giant child. She finds herself fitted into the curve of his arm so tightly that it's as if they are connected. So warm.

Worse: she has no memory of the transition.

Fixed in place, she goes scurrying around inside her head. She doesn't know *why*, but this is *how*. Fast. She left the house with Steele last night because she thought . . . Right. That he'd show her the path, tunnel, bridge to the rim and the territory beyond. The way out. Ned begged to come with, but she was so fixed on escape that she dropped off that porch and took off after Steele without a second thought. *Be cool, Ned. I'll come back for you. I'll get us out.*

She left him behind, imagining that Rawson Steele would mastermind the great escape. Instead he showed her into his massed cartons like a realtor, she thinks, trying to sell off an unwanted house. She sat down with him in his shelter, bent on learning what she could— OK, she was excited. Unbroken days of uncertainty interrupted by this abrupt, forceful man with his odd, don't-fuck-with-me eyes. Decisive, she thinks, unlike . . . Stop it, stop judging him! *Davy, if we ever get out of here, when we come home, I'll make this up to you.*

She sat down in that carton thinking to find out what Steele knows, but he wasn't giving anything away. Instead he tugged on threads that tighten in her gut even as she slumps against him, trying and failing to break the connection that keeps her in place. As though they are somehow related via two best friends who ran off to fight the Civil War. Who are the long-dead Hampton Poulnot and Archie Rivard to her anyway? Is this vibrant, psychological shape-shifter sitting *this close* a reliable narrator or what?

Desperately, she replays the sequence. The sweep. *A physical manifestation of powers working behind the scenes,* Steele told her as the machine rolled past, but he wouldn't say which powers, or what scenes. What did she think when it ended, that Rawson Steele would open up and spill his soul? At the end he signaled that it was safe to talk. She spoke first.

One question. All she did was ask him that damn question. She didn't want much. Just an answer. Then she'd know whether to trust him or not. *What were you digging for?*

She has no memory of what happened next.

Now they are here.

What happened in the long silence that he dropped into the space between them then? Did she fall asleep and this happened, or were they both gassed or poleaxed in a sneak attack? What force broke down their cardboard shelter, and who dumped them here? A flash of sense memory makes her shudder: her head bouncing against a dense, bony shoulder. They were carried here.

Or she was.

Drained by the long siege of dislocation and displacement, Merrill thinks, *They did something to us.* Unless it's simply that the air in the shed is cold and still, and the man by her side radiates heat. *I'm not weak, I'm just stupid.* God, she misses Ray. Ray would know what to do.

She tries to separate from him so she can stand, but her body won't respond. All her working parts are numbed, as though something put her whole body to sleep. *We were drugged.* Steele sits next to her with his head up and his back against the wall, and goddammit, she's still leaning against him— not for support— for the warmth, she supposes, thinking, *wrong.* Listening to his breath coming and going behind his teeth— that almost-whistle; she can almost catch the tune.

She needs to sit up straight, for God's sake, separate, but it's warm here and she's too numb, or is it drawn— *close,* she thinks, *oh, shit, we're sitting way too close*— to move away. There are things he said to her during that long night in the carton and things that have to be said. Yet here they are like a couple on a wedding cake, side by side. She needs to stand up and put the real question. *What were you digging up?* She needs to stand up, raise her fists and hammer the answer out of him with her fists if she has to, but she can't. Quite. Move.

OK, he doesn't need to know you're awake.

When he runs a light hand over her hair, she doesn't even twitch; she listens. A fragment of lyric comes back to her: *"I was born about ten thousand years ago . . ."*

Leaning, she studies the wood-frame interior through half-closed eyes. After weeks spent roving the faceless streets of the compound, going back to her relentlessly spare and aggressively clean house, she is surrounded by so many foreign objects that she can't identify them.

The shed where they sit looks like the costume department

for some makeshift country theater where kid actor-wannabes get together and stage *Little Orphan Annie* in the barn. Look at it long enough, and the jumble on the long wall opposite sorts itself out into masses of garments and personal effects, the kind you'd find in a thrift store or in the back room of a funeral home, but whose things are they, really?

How did they end up here?

The wall facing the one where she and Rawson Steele are parked like abandoned bikes is thick with ranks of clothing too rich and varied to identify at first. Garments hang on a rail that runs the length of the shed, fixed in brackets so not even the raccoon coats and officers' greatcoats drag the floor. Boots, shoes, sandals are neatly lined up on the floor below. The few bizarre outfits— costumes?— that Merrill recognizes range from fur-trimmed, obscenely grand velvets and brocades out of forgotten throne rooms to homespun dresses to timeless cotton shifts that she could have worn to work in Kraventown before the instrument of their exile snatched her out of her life and dumped her here. She sees masses of coats, capes, jackets too old to place in time, and the more items she can identify, the worse it gets.

Hats— everything from tricorns to a top hat that could have gone down with the *Titanic*— costume items from everywhen hang from pegs, with bags and costume jewelry carefully organized on shelves above, contemporary clothing mixed in with— dear God— rubber boots and sou'westers and beaded buckskins and early American colonists' gear, hip-length vests and buckled shoes, everything catalogued and ranked like the detritus of lost civilizations. Or lost tribes.

There's Steele's almost-whistle. *"There's things about me that you'll never know . . ."* That song.

Or lost colonies. Her heart stops.

He's done, but the lyric has invaded her head. Her throat closes and her belly freezes. It takes all the strength she has left in her not to groan aloud.

Then. *Wait!* The orderly ranks of abandoned eyeglasses and neatly shelved suitcases beyond the rack of discarded costumes could be the personal effects of . . .

No, Merrill, don't go there.

Shit! We're not the first people trapped here. Electrified, she sits upright.

"Are you OK?"

I moved! I can move! "I don't know!"

He clamps a hand on her arm. "Hush!"

Startled, she yips. "Ow! Let go!"

"Don't. They'll hear." In the harsh overhead light, with that scowl, he looks like a god hacked out of a coconut husk. "I think it's starting up."

"I said, let go! What's starting up?"

"Too soon to tell." Then, concerned: "Are you all right?"

Anchored by Rawson Steele, she tugs against him, jittering like a helicopter trying to take off. "I don't know what I am!"

"What you are is waiting," he says, and does not say why or what he means when he adds, "I think this will be over soon."

"What will?"

"It's hard to explain."

Fragment, song fragment, *"I know the secret of the sphinx . . ."* They sit without speaking until, as if he senses a change in her, Steele lets go. "OK, they're gone for now."

"Who is?" No answer. God, it's cold in here. Pressing her back to the wall, with her head up and her shoulders straight for once and no parts of them touching, Merrill asks, "Are you working for them?"

Wait! He looks hurt. Everything in him lets go— expression, tone, manner, when he says, "No. No Ma'am. I'm not."

But the rest of that line: *"Nefertiti told me so . . ."* "Who are you," she says, pressing. "Who are you really?"

He sidesteps it with the nicest smile. "Whatever you want to make of me."

"That's not fair!"

"Face it." He squints as though it hurts to allow it. "We're none of us who people think we are."

"Then who are we?"

That sweet, touching grin: "Ourselves. That's what keeps us going, you know?"

At least they're talking. There's no reason for her to trust Rawson Steele, but there's the tintype: two rebel kids. She's not sure she trusts him, but she likes him. No. She's drawn to him— echoes of *that boy in high school that you know is bad for you.* "OK, what are you really doing here?"

"Waiting, same as you."

"You know that's not what I mean. This place. You got here— how?"

"Same as you. Snatched up, whatever that was. Blindsided and thrown for a loop."

She thought she was getting somewhere with him but they aren't anywhere. It's infuriating. "If they're gone, why are we still sitting here!"

"Who says they're gone. Trust me." He reaches for her hand and she's grateful for the warmth. "It's safer."

"Safer than what?"

"Not sure."

She turns his hand over and leans hard on his exposed wrist. "Who are you, Rawson fucking Steele. Who are you anyway?"

He doesn't shake her off or try to pull free; he lets her hand stay where it is so naturally that they both forget about it. He answers willingly, disarming her with names as familiar as that tune, falling into the soft, down-home rhythm as though he learned it by heart forever ago. "I'm just Archbold Rawson Rivard, Ma'am, from the low country Rivards, although I grew up in the North." He adds, "Us Rivards left the territory after . . . It's been a while. But you probably knew."

"So you were named for him."

"If you want to think of it that way."

When she least expects it, the rest of the verse comes back. *"I've walked the whole wide universe, above ground and below."*

"Why'd you change your name?"

"Oh, Ma'am, Ma'am!" He sounds flat-out Southern now. Sweet Tidelands whine. *From around here,* she thinks, forgetting that she is no longer back in the here that she knows. Gentling her, or trying, he says, with down-home ease, "Nobody wants to be called Archbold."

"No. The Steele part."

Nice smile, even in the dismal lights from the LEDs overhead. "You don't always want people to see you coming." He sighs. "Our families didn't exactly part friends."

Like he knows something I don't know. It's sweet, but he's elusive. "Why are you here?"

"You mean *here* here? God only knows."

"That's not what I mean. I mean in Kraventown." Still sitting, she makes a half-turn and plants her hand in his chest, coming back at him again with the question that's hounded her ever since the night their lives split in two. "It's like you were hunting down something you could claim or build or take from us, and you never said what. What do you really want?"

This time he answers— more or less. "I just came looking for what's mine."

"Son of a bitch!" She is less angry than confused. "In my backyard?"

"Oh, Merrill, don't let it bother you." He removes her hand and puts it in her lap like an old-time Southerner returning a missing glove. "I was just digging up the rings. Two Citadel class rings, Ma'am, tied up together in a handkerchief and buried behind Russell Kraven's barn."

"That burned in the '90s. Eighteen nineties. But you knew."

"One way to end a property dispute," he says, leaving her to take it any way she wants. "Rivards are kind of famous for it. Milt Kraven subdivided the land where it stood . . ."

"And built my house. For a Northerner, you know a hell of a lot about us."

"Lady, it's all up there on the Web. Any damn fool could find it," he says easily, and holy hell, the cadencing is, what? Authentic. "The past is a powerful thing and yes Ma'am, it's crazy, but I took leave without pay and came all the way down to Kraven to find my Citadel ring."

My ring? "Like the secret treasure map's inside it or some other damn thing, like every crap novel I've ever read."

"This!" He slaps the floor and sand flies up. "This is not a crap novel."

"Sorry!" In the time it takes him to resume, Merrill gnaws the inside of her mouth, studies her nails, tries to shake the sand out of her hair. When he does speak, words come out of him all rough and ragged and at great cost, like the truth being dragged naked over rocks. It's such a relief to have somebody else's grief to think about that Merrill lets him talk on, and it's none of it anything she expected. She's been alone in this new, bleak life for so long that— stop it, lady. Don't.

The first words cost him. Coughed up like a hairball. "OK, before me, there was just . . ." He swallows hard and rethinks. "My mom was the last living Archbold Rivard's second v.p. in his holding company before she had me. You know, the one his great-great set up to handle the money he took from Luke Kraven in the property dispute."

She does.

When she doesn't acknowledge this, he goes on. "She was the last in a long line of pushovers, you know? One more sweet, deluded girl bowled over by the Rivard profile and the good old family name, so what does that make me?"

"His . . ." She stops before *bastard*.

"He already had a damn family. A whole 'nother family. Wife and two little girls stashed in Alexandria, big brick house with long wooden porches, right there on St. Asaph Street. I went and studied it, but I wasn't about to go in. His real true family, you can see where I am with this." He fixes her with those eyes that will not stay the same color. "So, the ring?"

Who are you? Squinting, she would like to reconcile this face with the tintype image, but Father threw it on the fire so long ago that she forgets. "The ring."

"It's pretty much all I'll ever have."

And all the breath in her lets go. "I see."

"So that's it." Steele's gesture reminds her of the time and puts her in this place, under the cold, colorless overhead light, on the cold floor with the sand sifting down at such a rate that she wonders whether they are even what passes for safe. Then he adds, "For now."

"Don't," she says. Because he's whipped them into an unbreakable circle, she slips into childhood rhythms to bring him down, "Don't do me like that."

"In the end," he says, "you might want to have Hampy's one.

They knotted the two rings in a handkerchief from Archie's house, two rebel officers, just kids."

"Oh, please!" Merrill gestures at the unseen and unknown forces beyond the shed, at everything inside the rim and everything above and below the surface of the desert floor and asks once more. "*What* are you?"

"What I am is, I'm stranded. Stranded and confused, same as you." He moves to take her hand, thinks better of it. "And fuck no, I have no idea how we got here."

"*Here* here?" Yes, she is goading him. "Or stranded in this damn desert?"

"Either. I was out cold when it happened, same as you."

"Out cold now, or back then on the first day we got here?"

"Both."

They are sawing back and forth and Merrill doesn't know how to make it stop. "How do you know I was out cold?"

"They do that. Gas. Go easy, Merrill Laneuville Maxwell Poulnot." *How does he . . .* "We're in here for the long haul and nobody knows how long that is or what it will turn into, so will you let it be? Just let it be."

. . . know these old names? "I have to know."

"Believe me, you don't want to know." He stands abruptly. Paces the length of the shed. "We can't stay here. We need to find a way out."

"I thought you said . . ."

He cuts her off. "In case."

Troubled, she gets to her feet. The effort is tremendous. Shaking her hands as if to thaw them, she scuffs the sand underfoot to start the blood moving and takes out after Steele, walking where he walks, going faster, faster as her blood runs higher and her muscles respond, pacing the length and breadth of the shed.

As they go she is thinking, thinking faster now that she's up and moving. "There's got to be a door. I mean, how else did we get in?"

"I don't know how we got in."

He either does know or he doesn't know; it's troubling. All Merrill knows is that where they are now, there's sand on the floor, sand in her hair, but no sand coming in through the tightly fitted planks in the walls. She looks up. "Me either," she says, "unless there's a hatch."

He says, too fast, "No way. There would be stairs," and busies himself at the far end of the shed.

Merrill persists, craning at the ceiling overhead as though she'll find daylight leaking in around the hatch. Afterimages from the LEDs blind her. If there's an opening overhead, it's hard to identify from here. How would they reach it?

Pile up all these suitcases from Treblinka and Manzanar, the clothes and belongings left behind by the Vikings who vanished in Greenland, the missing settlers of Roanoke, passengers on drowned ships, the lost tribe of Israel and all the other lost colonies represented here? Claw their way up the discarded shells of lost lives until they make it to the top?

Would that be sacrilege? Ray would know. She wishes to hell it was steady, dependable Ray locked in with her and not Steele, gorgeous and changeable as scenes in a kaleidoscope. She might not know where she was, but with Ray, she'd know where she stood. Steele is volatile, half dynamo and half wounded youth; she'd like to ask him about all this but he's distracted, rapping his way along the far wall, stopping to listen and moving on as though at some point it will sound hollow, and he'll find their way out.

There's a subtle shift, as though something big has begun to move. Startled, Steele looks up.

He groans, "Right." As if this is inevitable.

Seconds later she hears it. They are many, and they're running this way. The vibration sets off a little sandfall overhead. Merrill jumps back. The wooden ceiling of the shed where they sat for so long is indeed its roof, with sand coming in faster, revealing a square of light. The hatch.

"Rawson, look!" Her voice goes up in a little shriek. "Look for the ladder."

"Not now," he says, but she's too excited to care.

Never mind the growing mob-sound overhead. Merrill parts the heavy coats to feel her way along the wall behind. Shaking with excitement, she works her way along the clothes rack, parting hangers to see, closing the gaps and moving on to the next rank so fast that empty costumes go by like pages in a child's flip book. Hidden so cleverly behind a tier of fur coats that the maker thought she'd never find it, there is a ladder. She calls, "Over here!"

He hisses, "Shhh!"

The first heavy feet pound across the concealed roof above them, disturbing the protective layer of sand, but Merrill doesn't care. She wants what she wants. "I found the ladder!"

"Don't!" He is behind her in seconds, locking protective arms around her, swaying to keep her in place. "Be still. If they find us . . ." He doesn't have to finish.

She backs into him so they are clamped together, one on one, and stops. Whoever he is, whatever this is, it feels right. Now she is aware of footsteps directly overhead— too many, running too fast. "My God!"

A shudder runs through him. "If you pray, you'd better pray that they don't stop."

Possibilities chase each other through her head so fast that she waits, holding her breath until it hurts.

Then he adds, "This time. Hang in." His grasp on her is so steady, his voice so sure that she would do anything. "I think I can get you out before they come back."

22

Dave
Friday into Saturday

"I have to go back," Dave said when Earl put him down here in the back bedroom, filled with photos and trophies from some old war.

"Not while they're still out there. You got people after you." Earl pushed him into place on the bed like a medic on the battlefield and threw a blanket over him.

Dave could not stop thinking, thinking, thinking. "I'll need your raft."

"You'll lay low, asshole. When it's time, I'll carry you."

The long afternoon blurred into a long evening. Davy slept through most of it. The hard days' nights since he lost her piled up like boxcars in a train wreck and ran right over him. This is what it boils down to. He lost her. He lost Boogie too, and he thinks it was sheer carelessness.

Like this whole mess is something he did.

When he most wanted to light out and fix everything he'd done wrong, Earl warned, "Lay low," which he did in the Pinckneys' back bedroom, where no light came. Until the last cop car crunched down the road and the last of Poyntertown's knuckle-dragging supernumeraries crunched through the woods corralling off-islanders, there was no leaving this room. Earl's father slept here from the day he collapsed until he died of something

Theda wouldn't talk about. She closed the paneled storm shutters the day his eyes glazed over and he fell out, and when they brought him home from the hospital she put him to bed in here and closed the shutters for good. She locked them down with Gaillard Pinckney Three's fancy wrought-iron latches— proof against hurricanes and tidal waves, whatever came. Never mind that Earl was too young to divine the future as it pertained to his mother, particularly not the one Theda's mind is wandering around in now. His own mother, and he never saw it coming.

Maybe she did. As they took Felix Pinckney away she said, "When I look like I'm fixing to die, lay me down in there." That day she nailed the shutters tight so they would stay latched, as though anybody can batten down and keep death from coming in.

All they keep out is the light. An ideal place for Dave, short on sleep and looking like he does. Fuck, why didn't he grab his damn clothes out of the closet when he was back at Merrill's; he looks like a Necco wafer in Ray's things. Pastel store-dummy laid out on the bed in the Pinckneys' dying room in another man's clothes.

He left everything behind on Kraven, including Boogie Hood.

The dark, sad bedroom is like the Island of the Lost, lined with Felix Pinckney's books and photos from some old war— Nam, Dave thinks, although Earl never said. It's still just how he left it, probably because for Felix, it was the Last Good Time: one of those places where the past moves in to stay, getting so big that it crowds out everything else. There's no space in that room for unrelated objects— or for new thoughts, which Dave thought was fucking appropriate. With rednecks beating the bushes for him, followed by armed bounty hunters crosshatching the channel on Jet Skis, the dying room seemed like the right place for him.

Beached in the old man's bed, Dave tossed and sweated, hounded by possible futures. Scenarios flashed on and off like lights in a hurricane, never the same thing twice. The dead man's remote past was a lot easier to live with than whatever was going on out there— or what went on back then, before the stupendous . . . what?

Vanishment.

It split him in two.

Stupid bastard, whatever he and Merrill had between them before they parted company is pretty much wrecked— that sad, ugly last exchange, with no way to rewrite it or start all over again. Like a man in an old copper diving suit dropping over the side of the mother ship, he fled into sleep, sinking until the next damn fool tromped up on Earl's front porch or tried to get in by the back way hunting him, and the altercation brought him to the surface— aggressive fuckers, your redneck whites.

Life went on in the rest of the house as though Davy wasn't there. Earl kept busy pretending he wasn't. Outside, intruders came and went until they stopped coming.

He slept until Earl brought in a plate with corn bread and his best shrimp pilaf— when? It was either stone dark outside or not. It was midnight inside his head. "Perloo. Bored much?"

"Hot and cold running rednecks." Earl shrugged. "I had to look busy."

"I should go." With Merrill missing and whatever hopes he has for the two of them pending, he asked, "Is it time?"

"Not nearly. It's half past nine."

"I should . . ."

Earl took the plate from him. "Not yet."

"Earl, it's already fucking dark."

He was halfway off the bed when Earl stopped him with the flat of his hand. "Not now."

He snapped to, electrified. "There's someone in the house."

"Shuh, that's just a DVD." Earl pushed him back down on the bed. "I put on *The Wild Bunch* for Mom."

"You're some kind of ironist." He tried again. "Let go."

"Can't."

"Why not?"

They were beyond explanations. Earl stared Dave into obedience: *stay.* When he had him back in the bed Earl said patiently, "Not until the last patrol boat's come and gone."

"Patrol boat?"

"I warned you."

Dave sagged. "You did."

"And the motherfuckers are armed."

"OK, when?" Like a drowning sailor, he submerged with no memory of the last thing Earl said to him. He thinks the last and most important thing he asked Earl, that Earl never answered was, "How?"

This way.

They took the fiberglass flat-bottomed boat Felix gave Earl for his tenth birthday: a kid's thing, lightweight and easy for two men to carry. They stopped Earl's pickup a half-mile short of the Kraventown causeway and ducked under the boat without needing to discuss it. Raising it over their heads, they walked it the rest of the way, two grown men creeping down on the sand like a giant turtle, under the boat's scarred shell. When the lights swept their way they squatted, so they'd look like debris from an old wreck to whoever happened to be looking. They carried the boat out to the Kraven island bridge on the fisherman's path that flanked the raised road, pushed it into the water and shoved off. They rowed without talking, letting the current take them under the bridge and into the channel. They tied up under the dock in Kraventown harbor, waiting until isolated gunshots and the shouting died and it was safe to go on.

Early Saturday: Now

When they hear hollow footsteps overhead, the last designated sentry heading back along the dock to the street, they talk, but only a little bit.

Earl says reflectively, "So, what the fuck do you think happened here?"

And Dave is blindsided by the thing scuttling around underneath the wreckage in his head. *The plans.* He was so intent on getting here that he forgot. "I don't know what I think, I only know what I know."

"That being . . ."

The Northerner abandoned everything when he left that room in the Harbor City Inn. "I think Steele's behind it."

"Who?"

"I searched his room."

"Whose room?"

"Rawson Steele, or whatever the fuck his real name is."

"Who's that?"

"Crap developer, as it turns out, came in sniffing around all charming, but I knew. I saw the plans," he says, going on what little his Maglite showed him before he had to cut and run. "He's fixing to ruin Kraven, like the monster that shits on everything it's too full to eat. Giant water park on the lake, apartment tower, megamall, the works. He holds messes of deeds and shit. People you don't know about already sold out to him."

"I don't know much about Kraven," Earl says.

"I do. This dude's bought up half the property out there."

"Without you knowing?"

"Shills," Dave says. "He sent shills in to pick it up for him, and they got it cheap. Too bad he didn't scope the lake for himself before he sank all that money into it."

"The lake!" Earl smothers a laugh. "Wait'll he starts to dig."

Dave finishes, "In flood season."

"He'll be floating out to sea on the forms before they even think about pouring cement."

It's dark under here, but Dave knows Earl is grinning. The idea that anybody can do anything but grieve tugs him eight ways to Sunday.

Earl adds, "But I kind of don't think he could disappear a whole mess of people."

"He wants to get rid of us somehow." It takes him a painful while to say, "If it's him and I can prove it, at least we'd know where to start."

"What makes you so sure?"

"They're all gone, and besides." Desperation makes him dogmatic. "Everything happens for a reason!"

"Who says?"

Anger roars into Dave, *wham*. "It has to! There's gotta be an explanation."

"Like, scientific or techno?"

"Yeah."

Earl comes back after some thought. "Don't count on it. There's a lot going on that we can't see and a lot more that we don't know about," he says to Dave, whose life has marched in order until now.

"There's always a reason."

"What if God just did it for no reason?"

Dave goes all werewolf in the middle of the change; fangs sprout. "What makes you so sure there's a God?"

Gentling him, Earl tries, "I'm not sure about anything, but if you meet him, tell him . . ."

God. Dave is trapped in rage: can't get in, can't get out. Instead of picking up on Earl's favorite setup line as he has ever since fifth grade, instead of finishing with ". . . *tell him I have a colored friend,*" so they can both laugh and get over it, Dave cuts him off. "It wasn't God."

Good old Earl. "Fuck you know."

"I don't know what the fuck it is!" This is so true, so utterly obscene, and the truth of her disappearance is so irrefutable that it beggars him.

"Right." Earl's working hard to redeem the friendship. "We don't know how it happened, but it happened."

"Why?" Shaken, Dave thinks, *God! Why am I so bitter,* but in spite of this, unmoved by Earl's persistent kindness, he rears up and lashes out. In a fit of blind logic, he brings down his fist on Earl's knee. "Everything happens for a reason!"

Confident even in unknown waters, Earl says, "Face it, you may never find out why, or how."

And so scared. What if they never . . . "Shut up."

"Shuh," Earl says. "There are things we know and things we'll never know, get used to it."

"No!" He drives his fist into Earl's shoulder, too close to the heart.

"For true," Earl says. Earl, who is still easy in his life, repeats as though they're still friends, "So, deal with it."

Dave's voice is so raw even Earl flinches. "Just stop!"

"OK fine." Earl picks up the oars, starts to row. Gliding out from under the dock and back into the channel, he heads for the tidal creek on the east end of the island, where they can make land without being seen.

Dave lays silence between them like a knife. They're lugging the boat out of the water at the head of the creek when his voice comes back. Whatever he does on Kraven island, he'd better do it soon; sun's on its way up, showing pink over the horizon. Wading in through the sawgrass he says, too low for anybody but Earl to hear, "You could of left me off at the harbor."

"Fuck I could."

For too many reasons he says, "It would have been better. You'd be home by now."

"No big deal."

"I forget why you came."

"Boogie, remember? You felt so bad about him."

"Right."

"That's all. You get Boogie out and we take Boogie home, somebody has to do it. Then we're done." Earl waits too long before adding, "Maybe forever."

So Dave says what he has to, to make up for it. Picking up on the running gag Earl laid out when they were ten and just now, back at the city dock, the one stupid Davy blew off in a fit of rage, he feeds his best friend in the world the classic setup line. "What if I get busted?" It used to make them fall out laughing like bandits. Now it's a sword that cuts more ways than Dave can bear to think about but he tries, waiting for Earl to come back with the punchline that bonded them. Good old reliable, they used it to stir up trouble with the worst people:

Just tell 'em you have a colored friend.

But Earl is beyond comeback lines or anything else they've shared. "Take care, dude, and fuck you." Then he bends over the side of his boat, reaching under the seat. "Hold up, asshole, you forgot your shit."

Yeah, right. He's about to go up there empty-handed.

Earl hands off a chisel from the box his dad put under there when they were ten. "You might could stop a guy with this."

They're done talking. Dave nods and slips it under Ray's snakeskin belt. *Do this*, he thinks. No time for the blueprints in the hotel milk box. *Do this fast, so Earl can go home.*

His progress through back ways to Front Street is smooth, although he's making it at first light. The occupying forces have done everything they could and are sleeping it off somewhere; somebody trucked in a generator and there are lights in the Harbor City Inn. By this time the few armed monkeys left patrolling the streets are tired and slow, easy to dodge. As he comes out in the block behind Bay Street, Dave hears a thump-thumping that he can't make out, although it is familiar. He comes around through the alley behind Weisbuch's store and it comes clear: the metronomic thud of Boogie Hood, tied up somewhere and doing like he does when things in his life get beyond him, banging his head against the wall like that will make it stop.

He's not hard to find. For no clear reason, they put him in a portable jailhouse— Ray Powell's horse trailer, trucked in and hastily converted to the purpose. Ray's palomino racking horse Sherman foundered ten years ago. He fell behind the barn. Even the vet couldn't get him up. There was no hope for it, so they had to put Sherman down right where he fell. Ray loved that horse. He said Never Again, but he kept the rickety horse trailer back there, just in case. The plaque that says Sherman on it is still screwed tight to the bottom of the Dutch door, which someone has secured with a Kryptonite bicycle lock.

Dave climbs up on the back bumper and looks in through the top half of door where Sherman used to hang his head out when Ray and Junior had him at horse shows in Charleston and Savannah. Ray keeps Sherman's trophies on a shelf in the barn to this day, or kept them until the day he vanished, along with everyone else Dave cares about, Merrill Poulnot in particular.

Infuriated by the grillwork some vandal nailed over the opening to keep Boogie in, he pries it off with Earl's chisel and looks inside. His big friend is crouched on the floor with his back to the door, rocking back and forth on his haunches, making that reassuringly regular thud with his head. He bangs like the noise he makes will bring help or put him to sleep or transport him to another world.

"Hush, Boogie, it's me."

Boogie doesn't look up, he just keeps on thumping. Some asshole secured the bottom half of Sherman's door with that bicycle lock but maybe he can get Boogie out through the top. He'll do it, no problem, but first he has to get his attention.

"Yo, Boog?"

Yeah, right. Boogie keeps on doing what he was doing, as if he hadn't heard. A little louder. It takes him four tries. Finally he forages in Ray's pockets and throws a sodden cigarette lighter at him. Boogie turns that full moon face on him, dead white except for the red rings around his eyes. "Davy!"

"Hush."

He doesn't hush; he can't. In a thin, scared voice a lot smaller than he is, Boogie asks, "Are you OK?"

It's like a knife to the heart. "I'm fine, Boogie. Just fine." *Fuck, it's my fault you're in there.* "Can you stand up?"

Barely, but Boogie does.

Moving after all this time— how much time?— must hurt; his big friend is so slow and sad that Dave's heart breaks. *This is my fault. I never should have left you.* There's no getting this man out through the top half of that door, not like he is. OK, the hard way.

It's getting light fast. There are unknown quantities patrolling out there. He has to hurry. It's a sixty-year-old trailer. Layers of paint have glued the screws and the hinges to the wood. Patiently, Dave pries at the paint with his chisel until the paint cracks and the hinge starts to give. It takes too long but he talks nonstop, gentling Boogie in a low voice as he works until the whole mess, Kryptonite lock included, falls to the ground and the half-door follows, turning itself into a ramp as it drops, taking Dave down with it. He has to roll over and out from under before it pins him to the street, which he manages seconds before Boogie tramples out like a bolting horse and mashes him.

On this second day of the occupation, the streets leading back to the tidelands are quiet. Dave is wary and reflective. No invaders in sight, maybe they left off looking because they're done. Maybe two days of wrecking and pillaging wore the suckers out. Maybe this, maybe that, *get Boogie the fuck out of here while you still can,* which is a lot easier than he thought.

"Come on," he says to Boogie, hurrying him along.

"Where?" *Boogie, hush!*

"Tidal creek, now, shhh."

"Why?"

No more questions, please! "Earl's waiting with a boat."

"I'm hungry."

Shit, did they not feed you? "I promise, as soon as you get to Earl's house."

Boogie hesitates. "Off island?"

"Yep. I told you, Earl is out there with a boat."

"A boat?"

"Earl's carrying you to his house, where it's safe."

The big man slows down. "Off island. I can't."

"Boogie, you can't stay here." Boogie is too big to move if he decides to stop moving. *Say the right thing or he'll dig in.* "He makes the best shrimp perloo."

"But they won't know where to find me!"

"And corn bread."

Boogie, yearning to be diverted: "You sure?"

"Earl's corn bread is awesome, no shit. There's a ton left over. So, you're OK with this?"

To his surprise, Boogie nods. Relieved, he says, "OK."

Dave thinks to reassure him, just in case. "If the rapture comes, it won't matter where you are, Boog. They'll find you."

"Oh, that. I done gave up on that."

Stricken, Dave says, "I know what that's like."

From there on, they don't talk.

There are no false alarms and no real ones on their way out to the marshy tidal creek; at sunup they come out into the open and there's Earl poking around in the sawgrass where they beached his boat a lifetime ago. His oldest friend says, "Dude!"

OK, Dave thinks. *OK*. On a better day, he would be smiling.

Earl waves them into the boat. "It's getting late."

Hanging back, Dave gives Boogie a push in the right direction, into the shallows where Earl stands, waiting to get him into the boat. "No problem. Nobody's out that I saw."

"Boogie is bigger than I remembered."

"He's about the same. No problem, Earl."

"Shit yes it's a problem."

"I said, no problem."

With his back to the gaudy sky and the changing water, Earl hesitates, squinting. "Don't know if I can fit you both."

The grief and confusion that have been driving Dave since he lost Merrill eddy and fuse into the decision he'd already made without being aware of it, that solidified at some point in Felix Pinckney's bedroom just before night. He takes a breath. "You'll be fine."

By this time Earl has Boogie in the boat. "Hurry up, dude. We'll make it somehow. Let's shove this thing off."

"Sure thing."

Together they lean in and push until the boat clears the mud and at the exact right moment, Earl skins up over the side and into the bow like a diver surging out of the deep end. He settles in the bow, a perfect counterweight to Boogie in the stern. "Get in, let's see if this motherfucker still floats."

"Take care of him, Earl. I'm not coming."

"Hell with that. Get in."

"I was never coming," he says.

"We did what we come for, Ribault. Let's go."

The rest rolls in on him like an eighteen-wheeler. "I can't."

"Dude . . ."

"You knocked yourself out for me and I thank you, but. OK. I have to stay."

"What for?"

He is done grieving. "Just shove off and let me do this."

Earl is grieving now. "That won't bring 'em back."

"No. No, Earl, it won't."

"Then come on." Earl stands to make his point, never mind that the boat is rocking. "Come with."

"Sit down before I capsize you. Sorry." Still mired in the saw-grass, Dave gives the boat a last hard push. "Can't."

Earl's face says things he can't find words for. "Dear God, don't make me come back for you."

"No need."

"OK then, I won't." Earl ships his oars, reluctant to turn away. "But this obsession or whatever."

"It's not an obsession." It isn't even a need. It's a *want*.

A Gullah lilt to Earl's concern. "It's gone sink you."

"Chill, Earl. I am." Dave can feel the gangs of expressions snaking across his face, none of them fixed. "You'll keep care of Boogie for me, right?"

"Right."

"Now, shove off and let me do this, OK?" He will go to ground and pass the day somehow, blind and ignorant and uncertain, gearing up for whatever comes next. He has no idea what he is waiting for, only that it's something he has to do.

"Do what?"

"Whatever." The rest comes, but he doesn't say it. *I have to wait.* He says, "Now get the fuck out of here."

"OK then, but if you get busted . . ."

Oh dude. Oh, dude! Right. Part on the laugh line. "No prob, Pinckney. I just tell 'em I have a colored friend."

23

Merrill
Now

She can't even guess how long she's been waiting here at the bottom of the ladder with Rawson Steele holding her in place, unless he's holding her up. She doesn't like leaning against anyone for support, but they're stalled here until the last of the crowd milling overhead moves on and the last shout dies, and in their dank prison, she is grateful for the warmth. Knowing Steele— which she doesn't, really— she thinks he'll make her wait even longer, and she can't tell whether he's holding her here to prove he's in control or to keep her safe.

Without her here, would he wait? Would he even have to wait? He could still scramble up and abandon her, but he waits. For all she knows, he is one of them, keeping her in place until it's time. Question being, time for what?

Who were those people running along overhead?

In stasis, she thinks, *too many questions,* but she can't stop them coming. Does the hatch in the roof open on the glistening white compound she remembers, or will they come out on the broad, empty desert beyond the rim? She doesn't know. She doesn't know what country the desert is in, or whether there is in fact a fixed location or whether she's been abducted and abandoned in a state of mind. Time, facts, truth— everything is in flux.

She tugs, thinking to separate herself so she can think. "Let go."

"Sorry, I can't."

She wants to separate; she doesn't want to separate. "I said, let go of me!"

"Shh. Not yet."

Together, they stand, linked until the last sound above them fades away and he releases her.

Merrill turns on him. "What *was* that?" This is the question that troubles her on so many levels that she can't number them.

"I needed to be sure."

"That isn't an answer." She starts up the ladder.

He is abrupt, protective, kind. "No!"

She makes other false starts but each time he draws her back and oddly, this seems right. The last time she tries, something Steele hears or thinks he hears: a shout, footsteps returning, the clang of metal on cement— cement!— makes him yank her back so sharply that she turns on him, bristling like a terrier. "Stop that!"

"Shut up or you'll bring them down on us." He puts her aside like a chair accidentally set in his way.

"When?"

He turns as though she hasn't spoken and stalks the length of the rack of forgotten clothes.

She's too distracted to stay angry. Cement. Is there a road up there? The rim? What?

Steele drags an armful of overcoats off their hangers and drops them at her feet. "Sit down, OK? We'll go when it's time."

"I don't even know what time it is!" Merrill is anxious, hungry, pissed off, hungry, God is she hungry! In ordinary, more or less predictable life; in stories, where outcomes can be controlled, there would be mints in one of these coat pockets,

ossified chocolates in the nearest handbag or K rations in a hel-
met from some old war or compressed food packs shelved with
the astronaut gear. In the real world this rangy Northerner, her
protector or captor or whatever he is to her, would rummage
until he found her something to eat. As it is, they are adrift in
an unpredictable world where time ebbs and flows and nothing is certain, neither where she is nor how she got here while
Steele paces, thinking whatever he thinks.

Neatly folding an army parka that could have seen duty
in Siberia where so many were lost, he drops it on the floor
and sits so they are facing. Like a trained hostage negotiator he
asks in an easy, patient way, "Are you OK?"

Startled, she lets it all out. "I'm fucking starving!"

"Don't sweat it."

"It's been hours."

"Hang in, it won't be much longer." Either the artificial LED
light has changed or he has.

"How the hell do you know?"

For the first time she can see him clearly: kind enough and
worried, trying to gentle her. Saying with unexpected warmth,
"This will end."

"Sure. Sure it will."

"It will."

"What makes you think so?"

The next words come out in a groan. "Everything does."

This is so bleak that she finds herself rushing to reassure him.
"Not everything."

"Stories," he says. "Lives. What else is left at the end?"

"The questions." There it is. The challenge.

"No." An almost smile. "The mystery."

Underground in a place she doesn't know, in territory she
doesn't know with a man she understands she'll never really

know, Merrill gives up on answers. He's here. He's done his best to calm her and protect her; she's grateful, so she does as he says. She sits for so long that she forgets why she's sitting there, looks up to orient herself and finds herself looking directly into that changeable green gaze.

You, she thinks, drawn. Yes, drawn. *You, in this terrible place.*

This is when Rawson Steele surprises her. His voice comes up from someplace so deep that it's painful, just listening. It's been so long since they last spoke that she forgets what she said when the conversation died, but it's clear that he hasn't.

"Questions," he says as if they'd just left off. Then, as if this is a textbook quiz with the answers neatly filed in the Appendix, he says, "You mean, 'why are we here,' 'why this,' 'why us' kind of thing?"

"Exactly."

"It's not like they're lined up waiting to tell you."

She snaps to attention. *They.* "OK, Rawson. Who?"

Shrug: "Anybody."

"I asked you a question."

"Would it change anything if you knew?"

"Oh, don't!"

But he does. "Knowing won't change the end game." He is taking her somewhere she doesn't want to go. Like a tour guide, he puts her down and leaves her staring over the edge. Pats her in place with: "Nothing does. The only question is how well we play the game. Whatever it is."

"Oh, don't!" She wants to lunge across the few feet between them, grapple him to a safer place. "Don't be that person. Dammit, look at me!"

He is looking into his hands. After too long he opens his palms: that magician, fresh out of tricks: *Nothing to see here, nothing up my sleeves.* Quickly, he compresses them to fists so she won't notice that he's shaking. He is struggling with something. It takes him a while to get the words out. "There are things out there that we'll never know about."

"Don't say that."

"It's true."

"We still have to ask!"

"Oh, lady, forget it." Steele stands so abruptly that she rises with him. His gesture takes in their prison, the compound, the world and everything beyond. "Enjoy what you can and don't worry the big questions because nobody knows the answers. Really. Lady, let it go."

"I can't!"

Surprise: Steele nods. Patiently, he lays it out for her. "OK. There's a curtain between the natural and the supernatural. You know, there are things we can see and know, and things we'll never know. Every once in a while it twitches, just a little bit, so you'll know there's something going on back there."

"Rawson, make sense!"

"It's Archbold." Then he turns her around to face the ranks of costumes with a bright, astounding grin. "And this?"

It lands on her with the weight of the universe. The lost colonies, the unknown history, the fate of the legions of missing, which in the name of God she is right now, the missing who are never forgotten because nobody knows where they are or what became of them, the . . .

Realization overturns her. Missing. *Like me*. "What, Archbold. What is this?"

With a gesture wide enough to take in the known world, he says, "It's just whatever's behind that curtain," he says, grinning as though none of this just happened. "Moving, to remind us it's still there."

The weight is crushing her. She jumps up and runs for the ladder. "Oh God, I have to get out!"

"Wait!"

"I'm sick of waiting!" She grabs the sides and takes hold. The bottom rung is set too far above the floor for a woman her size to hoist herself up and get a foothold, but she tries again, falls back and runs at it a third time.

This time she is astonished by reassuring pressure on her elbows, the warmth of Rawson Steele's hands as he raises her up. She turns to thank him as she reaches the top, and the look they exchange then staggers her. Stunned, she hesitates, waiting for whatever comes next.

In the next second, he swarms past her on the ladder, "Wait here, on the ledge until I tell you it's safe. Look at me and promise."

She nods and he reaches down to brush her cheek, reassuring her with his touch. As he does so, his collar falls wide. Then he cracks the lid to the hatch, and the sliver of fresh sunlight strikes gold. She can see Rawson Steele clearly now, the concern in his face as he waits for her promise, two gold rings on a thong in the hollow of his throat.

He repeats. "Promise?"

"Promise." She would do anything for him.

24

Ned
Now

OMG, where is this thing going?

Wait. *What* is it?

All Father had to do was wave those awful scrubs. He grabbed the hoodie off me and used his bloody shirt for a flag. Everybody came out. Let one hundred people loose after weeks locked up in their crap white houses, piss them off and you turn them into something else. We aren't any of us who we were back on Kraven island; I'm not who I was yesterday. Shit, we are legion. Warning: Look out for me . . . It's wild! A solid hundred of us go charging along screaming, fit to break down the walls of this strange, dead city.

Tearing along like this, thud-thudding along the cement with *people I thought I knew,* I step out of Ned Poulnot like crap pajamas and leave that kid behind. I am the machine, packed in so tight with the others that we fill the street, ranks and ranks of us running along side by side by side and if I fuck up it won't slow this thing down. If I stumble, they'll catch me; if I black out they'll move in closer to hold me up without breaking ranks, until I come to; if there's a problem they've got my back and my front. The fast ones make the machine go faster and the big ones keep the little ones in step. Get out of our way or we'll march right over you and mash you flat. If somebody stumbles, even if one of the old, weak marchers drops dead we won't know it because we are a machine, and the machine rolls on. With the living holding up the dead there's no falling and no changing your mind. There's no getting off this thing and no stopping it so get out of our way! God, it's wonderful.

This is better than the game.

Fuck, it's nothing like the game. In the game I have power but when I disconnect I'm only me until I can get another connection. I can lay waste and pillage and kill people and eat a sandwich at the same time and never get hurt. If I get killed it's no problem, in the game players regenerate, so nobody really dies; if I get bored or hungry or too pissed off to play I just close my laptop and walk away, it's no big deal.

Behind all that slashing and killing, it's only a million bored or lonely people, typing. This machine we made is real. Father. Ray's blood on that shirt, his flag. Us. Locked in this thing together, until the end.

God, it's scary.

Father rises up on big old Delroy like a king steering his warrior stallion, trumpeting, "Kill him," and "Get Steele, get Steele," and here's the thing.

This machine he made of us is out to get Rawson Steele for what he did to Ray Powell whether or not he did it. We're out to get him for that and get even, string him up, shoot him dead, rip his head off, stone him into a bloody smear, after all he killed Ray, didn't he, the bastard stole our land and dumped us here, right? Unless he didn't. They're all angry, angry as fuck.

I'm not so sure.

I was there when Father came out of Ray's house all bloody and howling "Revenge," but he wouldn't let me see inside, so, truth? I don't know who killed Ray Powell. Father came out screaming Steele did it, but I was the only one on Ray's front walk today and this is what I saw. *Bloody handprints on Father's pants leg.*

Like Ray grabbed his leg, and Father kicked him off. So, Rawson Steele? I'm pissed at Merrill and him for ditching me last night, but I don't think he did it.

I think Father did.

I dig in my heels, going, "Wait!" but nobody does.

It's not like they hear. The liberation express roars on. There's a mess of cartons in the path ahead; the machine flattens them without dropping a beat, thud-thudding on, on to the outer limits of this cracked soup bowl like nothing can stop us. Fuck knows I can't even slow it down.

Then Delroy stumbles and the whole parade misses a beat, you know, that thing where your heart kicks in with an extra thud and you go *uh* because your breath just stopped? It's kind of like fate went Wuoow.

While the machine slows down to catch that breath you lost I lunge to the right, slip-sliding between the rumps of frustrated marchers and the fronts of pissed-off people in my row, sidling sideways, always sideways in spite of their mean, sharp elbows and bashing fists, until I'm almost free.

When Wayland Archambault scoops up Father before he can fall off Delroy altogether, I get my chance. He's riding high again, and his nightmare train can damn well leave without me. While Father cusses out Delroy for faltering, Wayland does the shouting for him. It sounds like a wild boar mauling a bear, *arrgh,* "Kill him," and they're off again, everybody but me, for I have popped out of the ranks like pus out of a boil. I go flat in a doorway as they go by, ordinary people Father turned into a hundred righteous assassins hup-hupping with glazed, flaming eyes and dragon-breath, screaming in a spray of snot and acid spit. *Kill him.* It's monstrous.

My guy Rawson Steele is Marked for Death and I'm too weak and stupid to let go of this doorframe right now because the truth just hit and sank to the bottom of my gut.

You were that.

Then I'm like, shit! Who doused the lights? Father started this thing around noon, like, an hour ago? It took time to bring everybody out and longer to get them moving; I wasn't running with them for all that long, but two seconds ago it got dark again and the streetlights went on. *Weird. So weird.* It's dead night here in the desert where your breath frosts over the minute the sun drops, but we were running so hard that I'm not cold.

Everything is dark and quiet now that Father and them are gone, like God or my sensei or the game designers or space aliens or foreign power that yanked us out of our lives and dumped us here want it dark for whatever comes next. From here I can hear that thud-thudding as father's engine roars on.

Then the moon comes up all quick and mechanical, like it's making a path to wherever I'm supposed to go.

That way. Down this road that leads out of the compound all the way to the rim.

Holy fuck, this is huge. Holy fuck!

After all the running and the pointless searching I'm at the edge of creation, with nothing but a belt of sand between me and the rim, and, wow! Out there the sand shifts and starts moving, even though there's no wind. Like it's sifting down into cracks in the shape of a . . .

Square. It's a trap door, and bingo bongo, the sun comes out like a spotlight on a stage set and I see . . .

Oh shit, Rawson Steele, coming up from underground. He looks around and hoists himself out to scope the horizon, making sure it's safe. He stands out like a panther in a kid's sandbox in those black sweats, even at this distance. I'm all, *Get down, stupid, they're after you!* but I'm so far away that he doesn't see. He's taking his damn time. From where he's standing, there's nothing to see yet, nothing to hear. He might not hear it, but there's a beginning vibration in the road, it's coming up through the cement, into the soles of my feet.

They're coming.

I have to warn him: *Get down, get down!* But if I yell, it will bring them. If he already knows they're close, he doesn't show it. Either that or he doesn't care.

If he knows they're out to get him, which is just about to happen, it's like, this is nothing to him. I jump up and down and wave my arms to warn him but he just stands there scoping the area between him and the rim. I strip off my shirt and start across the sand, waving it. Like anything will head him off. He bends double over the hatch, reaching down for— right. My big sister comes out blinking. Fucking Merrill, deer, headlights, that thing.

The breeze picks up and the sound of a hundred people yowling blows our way. I yell, "Get down, get down!"

Is he deaf?

Does he not feel the thunder in the sand?

Shit, maybe he does. Merrill rises up into his arms like a living statue and I love them for being here and being alive and looking so great together in the sunlight, but I hate them for being linked like lovers and exposing themselves just now; *I have to warn them,* I'm running, running hard with all hell coming up my heels and, yow!

They're here! The machine is here and it's too late for anything to happen except what Father wants, which is where this has been heading the whole time.

I am running flat-out, screaming, "Dammit, Rawson, fuck!"

Until the front ranks smash into me and knock me flat and

rage on, fixing to get Ray's killer and rip his head off and, on the way to the execution, stomp me into the sand.

Then something big— Delroy!— yanks me out of the mess by the hair *eeeyow* and, holy crap, big old Delroy Root picks me up like a baby and mashes me into his front and takes off, running back the way we came. We're thumping upstream, but nobody sees. They're focused on their target, coming down on him like a swarm of killer bees.

Delroy runs so hard and fast that my bones rattle and I lose it altogether and bury my head in his shirt. I was never part of the machine, I know, I was never Hydra Destroyer, I'm not even a man. I was only ever Ned Poulnot, going on fourteen. Finally, Delroy stops. He puts me down, sort of holding my shoulders so I won't fall over. "Are you hurt?"

I have to open my eyes. *Not really.* We are back in the plaza. "What the fuck, Delroy?"

But Delroy doesn't hear. He's watching them come pouring back into the plaza, the seize-and-capture happened that fast. He stands on the base of the flagpole and looks for Father, watching until Father rises up on Wayland Archambault's shoulders and waves that fucking bloody shirt. Then he jumps down. Turns out Delroy is Father's main man, and when you see Delroy coming, *look out.* He lifts my father off Wayland and sets him up on his own shoulders, like it used to was. At the base of the flagpole, Delroy puts him down on the high pedestal so Father stands high above the others, ready to tell us what comes next.

They are fixing to run Rawson Steele up that flagpole or stone him or beat the crap out of him, and they'll keep at it for a long time after he's dead.

This is confusing and terrible, Kraven islanders milling around in the plaza, still crazy from the hunt and crying for blood when there's too much blood splashing everywhere and I don't know whose it is because in the excitement, a lot of people got hurt. Eight guys grapple Rawson Steele up the steps to the flagpole where Father stands like King Solomon fixing to cut the baby in half. They back him up against the pole— which he takes to, good, strong knight on a pedestal with his head up and a proud, sharp look that says *fuck you all.*

Down below, Wayland Archambault has stupid Merrill clamped in place, although she's scratching and biting, and just before the execution or whatever, it gets unbearable and I break out. I can't fucking stand it. I run at dumb Wayland head-on and punch him in the nuts and he screams and lets go. Merrill wheels on him just then and rakes her fingernails across his eyes and before he can get them open, she breaks free.

It's so cool. My big sister is, like, blazing with rage so hot that the people around her back off and let her go; in seconds she's up there on the platform, plowing into Father, beating on him with both fists until he stumbles and falls off the step, which who gives a shit what happens to him then.

So my sister Merrill is right up there on the pedestal with my best friend Rawson Steele, what a rush! She's shouting to drown out the bawling, monstrous hate, but they don't hear. The mob surges up the steps, ready for the kill. Then Merrill, *Merrill Poulnot* lifts her head like Liberty and steps back until she's standing bang in front of our guy with her chin up and both arms spread, like that samurai goddess of war. Then everybody in the plaza understands— they can't mistake it— and it all goes silent. Then . . .

25

Dave

Alone out here at the edge of his world, Dave Ribault shudders. *There's got to be a reason.* Yeah, right.

Solitude has made him meditative. The last living human he spoke to was Earl, and that at the beginning of this long day. Since then he's been to the Harbor City Inn and found the milk box empty— no plans, nothing to show for his theft. He has used up the rest of the day cross-hatching the empty island, haunting other people's houses; he's rifled their kitchens and moved on without knowing what he's really looking for. He looked and kept looking until changing light marked the shift into late afternoon.

Now it's time to wait. Not sure where, doesn't know why, but he knows what he'll do next is wait.

After too long, he comes to ground; it seems like the right place. He's sitting on old Bill Deloach's overturned skiff here in the shallows, watching the tide go out. He's near the mouth of the tidal creek, where he last saw Earl. His best friend touched the bill of his crap baseball cap with that it's-your-funeral grin and headed out to open water and back into his life. Earl moved on with the keen, entitled look of a man who knows these waters so well that he can go anywhere he wants.

Dave watched his best friend and Boogie out of sight and thought: *Finally.*

He thought silence would put him into the right head, but it hasn't. After a long day of backing and filling, stymied in all the old neighborhoods— not skulking, exactly, just keeping low— he has returned to the marsh. Right. This is right.

All that conjecture, all this grief and he's no closer to understanding; he's looked everywhere and done everything and Merrill is just as gone. Not dead, just gone. Things happen and people deal with it and move on, but when someone you love goes missing, you're never done. The truth of it is, he realizes, when people vanish, the mystery lives on.

The one you lost and never find lives on forever, troubling the hearts of every soul she left behind.

This is just wrong. The power of lost colonies is that nobody ever knows why or how they vanished, or where they went. That famous one, almost five hundred years ago— where was it— Roanoke. Those people are long dead, but not. The Missing in Action in a dozen wars. Hundreds from that plane they never found. They're all still out there somewhere, he thinks: *like vanishing can keep a whole colony alive.*

He can't stop worrying the question. What happened? Is it something we did? Little Virginia Dare, the lost from the deserted *Marie Celeste,* no signs of a struggle, food on the stove, were their pillows still warm? The lost are eternal: still adrift on that raft, safe on some island or floating captives on a pirate ship. People die and you burn or bury them, but unless you know the outcome the lost live on and on, precisely because they never came back.

So, is Merrill eternal now?

The rest hits hard: *They never come back.*

What did Earl say? "There are things we know and things we'll never know."

Dave grieves, trying to imagine his life going on like this, the last Ribault hanging in here on Kraven island, getting old alone for no known reason. Merrill out there somewhere he can't go, living on and on. He's spent his life trying to create order in blueprints: symmetry on plots of land where there's no place to lay a straight line, blind Ribault trying to hold back entropy with his meticulous site plans, defying chaos with precision, uncertainty with design.

Now this.

The dead rock bottom. *What Merrill is, is, she's gone.*

Yes, he is circling the drain. All this looking for root causes and he still doesn't know.

You only thought you understood.

His shout is so loud that birds fly up. It surprises even him. "I'm sorry, Earl."

About the reason. This is less for Earl than for himself. *There is no fucking reason.* God he is depressed. With the day on the wane and everybody he cares about absent, he's not even sure why he's sitting out here exposed, so near the point. He thinks it's safe enough. The official presence has holed up in the bar at the Harbor City Inn. With nobody allowed on the island after foot patrols cleared the perimeter, the house to house search on Kraven island is done. He could just as easily go back to Merrill's house and wait for whatever happens next to happen, slouched in his favorite chair in front of the dead TV; he could wait comfortably in anyone's house or any vacation shack on the tidal creek at his back, but for whatever reasons he chose this spot where sawgrass gives way to water at high tide. Now he's sitting with his feet in wet sand with water creeping up on him.

The occasional surveillance plane, drone, helicopter buzzes over in the late afternoon light: military, news groups, every lookyloo with access to a private plane, but it's not like they're actually looking, they're just doing what people do. Every once in a while a Coast Guard cutter comes close, but from a distance, knowing what you can and can't see in the tidelands, Dave could pass for a log, a heap of mud. As though he has vanished from the face of the earth, but he hasn't.

He's here. Everybody else he cares about is gone. Now, where the fuck are they?

You're going along OK, pretty much set in your life, and then something like *this* happens. She's gone. They're gone.

Nobody knows why. It's a fucking mystery. All this thought, all this flailing and it's still a mystery, and right now he's alone with it, thinking, *What's the point?*

He sits on Deloach's upturned boat getting bleaker and bleaker until a flight of gulls takes off for the last time today. There's nothing in his life right now but the racket they make, departing, the sound of critters running in the marsh grass and the slap of the receding tide. That and the wish that he could look back up the creek and see somebody coming this way. He would be *so fucking grateful* even for one of the rent-a-cops to come up behind him and break the silence, clap a hand on his shoulder, anything to take his mind off this or, wait. Best-case scenario. Shoot him dead.

Dave Ribault is waiting. Waiting is all he is. Damn Earl, with his, "There are things we know and things we'll never know."

It puts him right back in college, with the math freak offering his take on Gödel's theorem of incompleteness: "Think of it as the hand reaching for the cup; it keeps reaching and the cup goes on receding."

Shit. He's been lost inside his head for so long that he comes back into himself with the roar of a felled ox: "Agh!"

Grief brings him to his feet.

Blinking, he turns, looking out over the water like any tourist waiting for the sun to drop; that's what normal people do.

So he is watching as something breaks the surface of the tidal basin— a pair of foreign objects at first then more of those . . .

Shapes, he thinks, gliding toward him in an odd formation, as though a school of fish has come into the tidal basin, more and more surfacing in a neat, geometric design— a triangle, or a wedge advancing, point first. At first the shapes look like domes, but as they glide into the shallows, the domes become heads and then the shoulders emerge and then bodies, more and more showing, dozens surfacing to march in like a legion of dreamers unless it's an advancing army, then, my God!

It's them.

As they approach, Dave is struck by the configuration.

Wait!

Just as he was acknowledging his loss and learning to live with it, Merrill Poulnot emerges, whole and drenched and radiant. She is in the lead— does she see him? Never mind! He heads for the water, floundering in an attempt to run through the mud. He's so slow, he is too slow!

Then the apex of the triangle sorts itself out into two figures, not one. Advancing through the water smoothly, like dancers, she and Rawson Steele are linked.

Not missing. Not forever. They are this. Here.

Years will pass before overt and covert government agencies, journalists and ambitious writers of every kind, psychologists, anthropologists, historians and voyeurs leave off grilling bemused Kraven islanders, but none of them seems able to recall or recognize the mechanics behind their mysterious disappearance or remember even the shape of where they'd been or what happened to them while they were gone.

Mired in the mud, stolidly watching the— approach, Dave grieves for everything he's lost. He will do whatever it takes— he'll do anything to get her back.

Acknowledgments

Every novel has to start somewhere, but I'll begin with a brief historical note. Back in the day, some ten years after David Hartwell turned up at Wesleyan for an SF event I'd organized, I met John Silbersack in David's office.

Like all the others, *Where* started inside my head, and grew with the encouragement of Joe Reed, my traditional first reader and live-in cheerleader. The first draft passed through the hands of novelist Kate Maruyama, a born story editor with narrative skills sharpened by years as a development exec in Los Angeles. I owe a lot to this most excellent friend and colleague, my daughter. And to Ko Maruyama for *Gaijin Samurai* expertise.

Thanks to Marco Palmieri and Christopher Morgan at Tor for helping all this happen, and thanks to Erhard Konerding, Documents Librarian, and Alec McLane, Music Librarian and Director of World Music Archives, for inside information on the music scene.

Now, back to the future: My special thanks to John Silbersack of Trident Media for his enthusiasm and his close, perceptive readings, and to David Hartwell for all of the above and for publishing, boosting and hanging out with us ever since the early seventies. I thank my stars for the alchemy that brought the three of us together.

Two friends, both named in this volume, noted the central obsession that drives it, a thread that runs through much of my fiction. One knew the backstory, the other did not, and I'm adding this story by way of explanation. *Where* unfolds in the narrative *now*. It's set in the South Carolina low country and in the desert compound, with characters you know by this time— well, all but one of them. "Military Secrets" unfolds in the same world as the novel, but with a different cast, and a setting that morphs as you read it, and yes, I use a first-person narrator. The story, first published in *Asimov's Science Fiction*, identifies the obsession— no, the engine that drives this novel.

— KR

MILITARY SECRETS

When the first bell rings, Mother Immaculata marches us outside for a special announcement. We have to line up on the playground according to size. While the taller kids file into rows behind us, we shuffle in place, wondering.

What is this, anyway? That "special," attached to "announcement." Will it be a surprise day off? Games instead of times tables or just ice cream at lunch? Maybe it's a field trip, orange busses lined up to take us all to Water World? Or . . .

My gut stutters. The biggest thing.

Then Mother Immaculata says, "Everybody whose father isn't dead, take one step forward," and everybody in the front row steps forward but me.

God, don't make me throw up.

She repeats the way nuns do, in case you didn't get it. "Jessie, I *said,* everybody whose father isn't dead . . ." Then she drops her arm like a starter's flag. Our whole long row marches off the playground and up the ramp into the gym. I can't.

I have to stay where I am with the second row running up my heels. There are more kids lined up behind them, row after row, up to ninth grade. Even Mother Immaculata is impatient, but I can't move. She comes down on me so fast that her big fat rosary rattles. She grabs my shoulder, hard and turns me around. "See that?"

It's a square of red tape laid out on the tarmac next to the bleachers. "Yes, Stir."

She gives me a push. "Into the box."

He isn't dead, I just don't know where he is, OK? "Yes, Stir."

For a long time, I'm the only one in the box.

When I was nine, the doorbell rang in the night. I went running down, but Western Union was gone. There was more in the telegram than she ever told, but I didn't know. That night she said it was just Uncle Forrest, investment things, now go back to bed. She waited until morning to tell me anything at all.

I was eating my cornflakes in the sunshine when she began. The Navy thinks Daddy's missing in action, she said, Don't worry, eat your breakfast, it's probably a mistake. I think she said, It says they just lost track of him, that's all, but she never explained. Then she went back inside herself and slammed all the doors. Daddy was "missing," she told me every time I asked; that's all she said.

I had to wait until she died to read the telegram. After the funeral I went through her things, which you do when your only mother dies. I found letters she wrote to the Navy Department in the same carton; carbon copies, neatly stored. When the Navy declared he was officially dead, she kept writing. She followed up on rumors, reported sightings, fresh details from classmates who had made it home; for decades she numbered reasons to believe **MISSING** meant exactly that.

Lost means they will find him, right?

Right.

This is how kids think. It's how I thought.

All the telegram said, Mother told me the next day, was that they didn't know where Daddy was. She finally got up and put on lipstick the day after: she said, Don't worry, they're out looking for him right now. I wrote the rest inside my head every day after that. His nice new submarine could be silent running, he's out there, but it's a military secret. He'll come back and tell us all about it. Unless he's on a desert island somewhere— accident at sea, he and his crew are stamping SOS into the sand— unless they're bobbing on life rafts because something hurt the sub. Living on fish and rainwater. People in books did that, and Americans in prison camps gave their name and rank and serial number and they never gave in. Skippers helped their men no matter what the guards tried on them, they worked together to escape. He and his crew could be tunneling out right now, crawling on their elbows through deep sand. If not, we would go in and rescue them as soon as we won the war.

Three weeks after we got the telegram, the mailman brought us letters from Daddy, and, look. They were postmarked two days after Mrs. Simpson struggled up our front steps with her sympathy casserole. First proof.

He's still out there.

. . .

It was only Thursday, so I made peanut butter and jelly on saltines and went to school.

When you're little, missing in action means a lot of things; the one thing it doesn't mean is dead.

They're out there looking for him, right?

So I went into Sister Marcella's room like always and sat in my same desk in the back, between Teeny Shail and Betsy Braswell. We ate on our same bench by the lunchroom window, and I didn't talk about the telegram, so they didn't have to know. See, officers' children don't cry. When he left for California I felt awful, but officers' children don't cry, not even when you can't see. He's counting on us to be brave. Besides, for all I knew they were finding him that very day, pulling him out of the water while I messed up long division or copied the names of the state capitals off the board. After the last bell I ran all the way home. It would be over and the kids would never even know.

Mother would come running out to tell me they made a mistake and we'd have waffles and cocoa to celebrate.

Instead it was big old Mrs. Simpson from across the street with a casserole, she was on our front porch, sniffling. She could hardly wait to say You poor thing, and she got upset because I wouldn't cry with her and I didn't let her inside. I had to take the casserole to make her go away. Mother was still in her room with the shades down, *Don't bother me*. She didn't come out for supper so when it got dark I had casserole and went to bed because tomorrow I had school.

Next day Sister Marcella popped out of the double front doors at St. Paul's too fast, like she'd been lying in wait. She knelt down in the middle of the sidewalk right in front of me so I couldn't get past. Kids started piling up behind. I guess she wanted to hug, but this dry cleaning smell came up from her habit along with other smells so I couldn't. Her face kept sliding around. *Oh, don't! Sister Marcella, don't cry.* Thank God she didn't. It was just an almost, which was good. Then she opened her mouth and words fell out. "Oh you poor child, you've lost your father," like it was something I did.

Then she pinned a Miraculous Medal on my collar and told me to be brave, right out where everybody could see. Kids stared, all but the ones that wouldn't look at me.

The Friday paper was on the bulletin board so it was the first thing everybody saw. His picture was up there on the front page. It didn't make it true, but now everybody knew. I don't know why it made me feel guilty. You just do.

I got through the rest of that year thinking, *If one more kid in our school got the telegram, at least there would be two of us, but that year, nobody did.* Hope made me savage. In fifth grade, I thought at least one transfer kid would come and I'd see it in his face. He'd walk into our classroom and we'd both know and I wouldn't have to be the only one. I hated it. Other kids' fathers got blown out of the sky or shot dead in combat all the time and our school would have a Mass for him, but we are not the same. When they tell your mother that he's Killed in Action, at least you know.

Missing is still out there, no matter what they say.

You miss him every day. Even after you find the telegram she kept: **AND PRESUMED DEAD** you play out the possibilities. You think, One day he'll walk through that door. You keep thinking it long after you look up and do the math. You're the exact same age he was when he got lost. Older, then much older, but still . . . Then you consider what time has done to him, what he looks like now and what he needs, but that's OK. You won't care what he looks like or how hard it is, when he walks in that door you'll be glad. You spin out the years thinking, *I will take care of him.*

By the time Mother Immaculata was done that day there were three of us standing in the red tape box, watching the ordinary people follow Mother Immaculata back into the building, row on row, leaving us exposed— two big kids from the middle school: this girl Dorcas and Bill, who's tall as a tenth grader, and me.

At the top of the ramp Mother Immaculata sees the last row up the ramp and back into regular life inside. Then she turns and gives us a look. We shuffle, not exactly looking at each other, frightened and excited— *You too!*— and ashamed because we're both girls but we're nothing alike, gaudy Dorcas with your uniform skirt rolled way up above your knees.

No. We are alike, we just didn't know.

Mother Immaculata doesn't say our names, but we can feel her eyes on us. We have our orders. "You wait."

Either the tarmac grows or we shrink.

When the doors shut on the mother superior her building goes away, leaving us three alone on the playground. For reasons. There's nothing in sight to remind us where we are, which town in what state, or even what country. There's just us three eddying on the tarmac, and at the far end of the playground, a bus. Did that bus pull up while we were watching Mother Immaculata direct traffic away from us, or has it been out here the whole time?

It's a gray steel cylinder with darkened windows, sleek as a bullet and all of a piece, everything tightly sealed until we're close enough. Odd: it hasn't moved. Neither have we, but here it is. The doors pop open.

It's for us.

We climb on board, in hopes.

The doors whish shut on our heels and the motor starts before we can make it up the steps, but you get used to that. When you're a kid you can't ask for explanations. You do as you're told.

The inside of the bus is even darker than the steely shell. As we come up the steps Dorcas tries, "hello?" Nobody speaks. We blunder down the aisle all pardon me, excuse me, looking for seats. Nobody moves, even when Bill fake-loses his balance and bumps them so he can fake-apologize.

We go along in the dark, following beads of light in the floor to our seats in the very back row. It's so dark in here that we can't make out who the others are, only that they're kids and they won't talk to us. Whether they're asleep or drugged or just pretending is never clear. We'll never find out where these kids were or what they were doing when they got picked up or why they were picked up in the first place or why we're all in here together, although I can guess. That's OK, I think as we stumble into the back row, but I hate that it took us forever to get here, and these are the last seats in the bus.

And that there are so many people in here. From the outside the bus doesn't look that big, but there's no bus driver to steer by, no teacher herding us, nobody to ask. When you grow up without explanations, you don't ask. You keep doing what you have to do.

As if he is watching. In hopes.

Days go by, at least I think it's been days. Food happens, I think, but I can't know if it really does. Sometimes the bus fills with the smell of food, people farting, shifting in all the rows ahead of us, but the only ones I hear talking are Dorcas and Bill and me, and only a little bit. It's questions, like why they won't talk to us and when is the food, although we never get hungry. The bathrooms are right across the aisle from us, but nobody comes and I don't have to go.

As we ride along we wonder, but we don't really want to know. It's enough to be running along ahead of the sad outcasts we were in the last place. Every few hours or days Bill or Dorcas will ask where this thing is going and we name places we used to live and places we want to see, just not the one we really care about, in part because we don't know exactly where that is. We don't ask each other who we're looking for because that's too personal, but we all know why we're here.

All the regular kids went back into the building that day, everybody but us. I think the war orphans left that place shortly after the telegram came to their house, unless the service sent somebody to break the news. Poor kids, their fathers got killed, this won't make it better but at least they know. And the rest? Ordinary, so they belong at St. Paul's. His job was essential to the war effort on the home front or he was too sick to serve; either way he didn't have to go. Either he never went to war, or it ended, and he came home, we don't know.

I know that they made Dorcas and Bill and me wait in the red tape box because we don't belong in that school.

There is no real place for us. Mother Immaculata thought one thing, but we know another. *Not dead.*

They just don't know where he is, is all.

So here we are parked side by side by side in the back row of the bus, sitting in here in the dark and it's nothing we did, it's who we are. Then the silence gets too heavy and we talk. Or I think we do.

Bill starts. "So where were all the kids whose fathers did get killed?"

"What?"

"You know, back on the playground."

It comes out of Dorcas in a wail. "I don't know, I Don't *Know*."

I do. "They don't go to our school."

"Oh."

Bill pushes: "Is that better or worse than this?"

Dorcas is quick. "Oh, it's much worse."

Not me: "I don't know, I don't *know*."

Change the subject, Jessie. Change it fast, but don't ask the next question. It's too personal. Never ask us where we were when we got the telegram.

Don't make us tell you what that was like.

I ask the question that it's OK to ask. "Where did they say he was when it happened?"

"Chosin." It comes out of Bill like a cough.

Dorcas whips her head around, all puzzled. "What's that?"

"You don't know?"

I think, but do not tell her, *Different war.*

Bill turns to me. "Yours?"

"Coral Sea."

"Where was yours?"

Dorcas finally gets it. "Manila Bay."

We all do. Bill stands up and yells at the backs of a hundred heads on the unmoved, unmoving bodies slouched in seats ahead of us because they got on the bus before we did. He yells loud enough to reach everybody in every row all the way to the front of the bus and Mother Immaculata and all those ordinary kids back at our old school.

Shouting, "Where did they tell you they lost him?"

And the answers come from every row, all the way to the front of the bus. When they do, it is stupendous.

"Tikrit," and "Manassas," "Da Nang," "Belleau Woods," "Benghazi," "Agadir . . ."

The names of all the old wars and certain new ones and wars we haven't heard of yet come out in a blast, cries that go on and on, as though whatever the nail is, Bill hit it on the head.

For the first time the bus stops.

Ahead of us, the others cough and shift in their seats, embarrassed. Reassembling themselves. There's the confused stir of someone standing, way up there in the front of the bus, followed by the doors whishing open, the hush of footsteps stifled as the thoughtful person or people hurry down and out. Then the doors whish shut and clamp tight so we can shove off.

In the back row the three of us scramble to change places, shuffling ourselves like a deck of cards so we can take turns craning at the window, but there's nothing to see. It looks darker out there than it is in here. The bus is moving again, everything dark and everybody silent, sending the three of us back into our own heads where we sit, curled up tight around our hopes. The bus stops again, long enough for someone new to get out. It's probably time for the third row to line up at the exit, but at the next stop, nobody leaves. I don't hear that gasp the doors make when they whish open, or the rush of somebody pounding down the steps, which is a puzzle. At least nobody gets on.

At the next stop so many people get off that I can't count them and all my blood backs up in my head: *Me next, me, me!*

Dozens get off and nobody comes back. A good thing, I tell myself. It could mean . . .

Oh, Jessie. Don't.

But the next time we stop kids seem to get off in no particular order, from the front of the bus, the middle of the bus, any-where in the bus; they scatter before the doors clamp shut on their heels while the rest of us ride on, and I begin to think . . .

I don't want to think.

Bill says it. "We're never getting off this fucking bus."

If John Paul Jones had a wife and kids that he left behind to fight for whatever; if he never came back, they're probably sit-ting up there in the dark somewhere near the front of our bus. Waiting. We aren't all the same age, in fact we're nothing alike. We are none of us the same person. What we are is people whose fathers got lost in some war, frozen at the age we were when we first heard. It won't matter when this happened to us or which war, the only thing that matters is, lost can mean anything. No matter how long you live or what they tell you later, he's still out there and— you mull the unfinished sentence as you run on, listening for the rest.

Author's Note: I've carried the story of the *Marie Celeste* in my head since I was, oh, ten, and first read the story. She was discovered adrift in the open sea in the late nineteenth-century— everything shipshape, gear neatly stowed, food on the stove and dents in some pillows to suggest that lives there had gone on undisturbed, until . . .

Seamen boarded the ship and discovered that with no signs of violence or disaster, all hands had vanished. The thing about the missing— lost colonies from the Roa-noke Colony to the passengers of jumbo jets that are never found and servicemen declared Missing in Action— is that they're never really gone. They don't leave any-thing behind, no physical clues to the disappearance, no cryptic notes for history to decipher, not even truncated last transmissions or black boxes, no bodies, translated: no proof of death. *At any minute they could walk through that door.*

In a way, the missing never die. Like all lost colonies, like all those lost servicemen, like every loved one who vanished without a trace to prove otherwise, *They're still out there.* —KR

About the Author

Kit Reed is the author of the Alex Award–winning *Thinner Than Thou* and many other novels. She has been nominated for the World Fantasy Award, as well as the Shirley Jackson Award, and has been a James Tiptree, Jr. Award finalist. She is also a Guggenheim fellow. Kit Reed lives in Middletown, Connecticut, where she is the resident writer at Wesleyan University.